GRANTA

12 Addison Avenue, London W11 4QR | email: editorial@granta.com
To subscribe visit subscribe.granta.com, or call +44 (0)1371 851873

ISSUE 160: SUMMER 2022

PUBLISHER AND EDITOR	Sigrid Rausing
DEPUTY EDITOR	Luke Neima
POETRY EDITOR	Rachael Allen
ONLINE EDITOR	Josie Mitchell
MANAGING EDITOR	Eleanor Chandler
SENIOR DESIGNER	Daniela Silva
ACTING SENIOR DESIGNER	Theo Inglis
ASSISTANT EDITOR	Lucy Diver
PHOTOGRAPHY EDITOR	Max Ferguson
COMMERCIAL DIRECTOR	Noel Murphy
OPERATIONS AND SUBSCRIPTIONS	Nellie Anderson
MARKETING	Simon Heafield
PUBLICITY	Lamorna Elmer, Pru Rowlandson, publicity@granta.com
CONTRACTS	Isabella Depiazzi
ADVERTISING	Renata Molina-Lopes, Renata.Molina-Lopes@granta.com
FINANCE	Robin Mackay Miller, Elizabeth Wedmore
SALES	Phoebe Llanwarne
IT SUPPORT	Kieran Spiers, Mark Williams
PRODUCTION ASSOCIATE	Sarah Wasley
PROOFS	Katherine Fry, Jessica Kelly, Jess Porter, Francisco Vilhena
CONTRIBUTING EDITORS	Anne Carson, Rana Dasgupta, Mohsin Hamid, Michael Hofmann, A.M. Homes, Hisham Matar, Adam Nicolson, Leanne Shapton

This selection copyright © 2022 Granta Trust.

Granta, ISSN 173231 (USPS 508), is published four times a year by Granta Trust, 12 Addison Avenue, London W11 4QR, United Kingdom.

The US annual subscription price is $50. Airfreight and mailing in the USA by agent named World Container Inc., 150–15, 183rd Street, Jamaica, NY 11434, USA. Periodicals postage paid at Brooklyn, NY 11256.

US Postmaster: Send address changes to *Granta*, World Container Inc., 150–15, 183rd Street, Jamaica, NY 11434, USA.

Subscription records are maintained at *Granta*, c/o ESco Business Services Ltd, Wethersfield, Essex, CM7 4AY.

Air Business Ltd is acting as our mailing agent.

Granta is printed and bound in Italy by Legoprint. This magazine is printed on paper that fulfils the criteria for 'Paper for permanent document' according to ISO 9706 and the American Library Standard ANSI/NIZO Z39.48-1992 and has been certified by the Forest Stewardship Council (FSC). *Granta* is indexed in the American Humanities Index.

ISBN 978-1-909-889-49-1

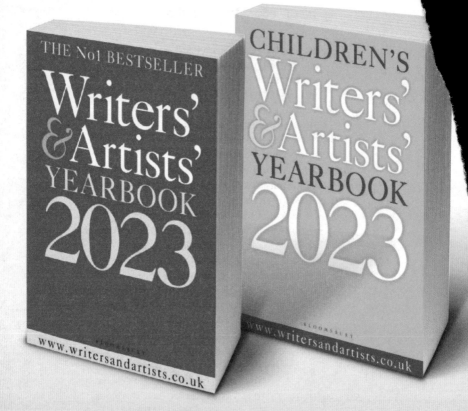

CONTENTS

Introduction
Sigrid Rausing

Letters from Ukraine
Lindsey Hilsum

29   **I Am the Word for God and Boy**
Aidan Cottrell-Boyce

41   **The Recipe**
Rebecca May Johnson

62   **Poppy Promises**
Thomas Duffield

91   **Skromnost**
Janet Malcolm

105   **Talk America**
George Prochnik

113   **The Moving Target of Being**
Suzanne Scanlon

134   **Debt Economy**
Rae Armantrout

136   **A Place that Belongs to Us**
Daniel Trilling

150   **Baghdadland**
*Aline Deschamps,
with an introduction by
Rattawut Lapcharoensap*

171   **Fatty**
Dizz Tate

185   **But the Heart in a Sense Is Far from Me Floating Out There**
Peter Gizzi

187   **Fateha**
Sana Valiulina
Trans. Polly Gannon

197   **Signs of an Approaching War**
Volodymyr Rafeyenko
Trans. Sasha Dugdale

202   **Having Recently Escaped from the Maws of a Deathly Life, I Am Ready to Begin the Year Anew** *and* **Figs**
Sandra Cisneros

207   **Fault Lines**
Jane Delury

219   **A Wolf in the Forest Wants**
Sarah Moss

231   **Notes on contributors**

Introduction

When we began to put this issue together, the course of the Russian war of aggression in Ukraine was still uncertain. As we go to print, some 15,000 Russian soldiers and several thousand – it's not known how many – Ukrainian combatants have already died. Up to 14 million Ukrainians have fled their homes, including the 6.6 million who have left the country. Most have gone west (over half are in Poland), but nearly a million people have been bussed over the border to Russia, voluntary and involuntary refugees processed and dispersed to halls and schools across the country. Many people have fled Russia, too, in the wake of Putin's hardening repression, temporarily or for good.

Most of the refugees are likely to eventually return (many already have), and cities will, I suppose, be rebuilt. But Putin will be remembered for war crimes, kleptocracy, and a grandiose and vacant ideology of aggrieved nationalism, military hubris, patriarchal orthodoxy and brutal homophobia. By the time you read this, things will look different again. We might have peace. We might have been drawn into war. Or – most probably – the conflict will develop into something in-between, a prolonged and inconclusive war turning into a running sore of global politics.

In this issue, Sana Valiulina reminds us of the Molotov–Ribbentrop Pact, the Soviet–Nazi agreement to carve up Eastern and Central Europe between the two would-be empires. *Channel 4 News*' international editor Lindsey Hilsum's 'Letters from Ukraine' gives a rare insight into war reporting from behind the scenes – lodging where you can find it, air raid sirens, international colleagues, the serendipity of good interviews. Journalist Daniel Trilling collates fragments from his interviews over the years with refugees from different war zones, to reveal, with the greatest of gentleness, the condition of exile. Volodymyr Rafeyenko, Ukrainian writer and poet, was in his home, a borrowed dacha near Kyiv (he and his wife had fled once already, years ago, from the conflict in Donbas), when the invasion began. Shrapnel and shells fell on roads and gardens. First the internet connection failed, then the electricity. The Rafeyenkos fled, with difficulty, and later found out that civilians ad been executed in a village not far away. In time the history of this war will be written, and what feels like one man's brutal fantasy will no doubt be revealed to have multiple causes, long- and short-term. But the ultimate responsibility for every broken body, every bombed-out street and building, every refugee, is still Putin's.

Our theme of conflict is internal as well as external. Janet Malcolm's text is about her mother, and her complicated maternal love. The family fled Czechoslovakia in 1939, and only fragments of their social world survived. This extract, as steely and insouciant as Malcolm herself, is taken from her last book, *Still Pictures*, a posthumous memoir.

Suzanne Scanlon writes about her breakdown when she was a student at Columbia in the early 1990s, followed by a long stay on a psychiatric ward. She describes the pressure to 'remember' abuse that never happened, in accordance with the then prevalent notion that severe mental distress, particularly in young women, was likely to be caused by early sexual abuse, subsequently suppressed and forgotten.

Sarah Moss lucidly describes a recent episode of anorexia. She fell into a mode of relentless efficiency, running mile after mile, working hard and cooking organic meals for the family while hiding her deeply serious illness from them. All the virtues of thrift, of 'up and doing', of healthy cooking and exercise fed into a compulsion beyond her control.

Jane Delury's short story 'Fault Lines' is about intergenerational eating disorders, in prose deceptively quiet. How come, in an issue on conflict, the writing turns so quiet? Not so, however, in George Prochnik's piece, 'Talk America'. Trying to make ends meet as a writer, Prochnik worked for a while for an American catalogue company. It was his unenviable task to man the complaint line, managing the enraged customers who were told that they had to spend *more* money to send back whatever useless thing they had bought, when the bulk of the price was postage and packaging in the first place.

This spring I lost my closest friend, Swedish writer Johanna Ekström, to cancer. 'Hold on to the afterlife of the beloved, it's the only thing / that's yours', Peter Gizzi's poem in this issue begins. I hold on, I realise, to an image of Johanna's afterlife. She is with my father. He, like her, was a resolute and irreverent atheist, and see them outside, in some sunny meadow, talking, laughing, deeply content. I can't quite hear them, but I can see the wind on their faces, a summery breeze.

'Having Recently Escaped from the Maws of a Deathly Life, I Am Ready to Begin the Year Anew' is the ironic title of one of Sandra Cisneros's poems. It's a celebration of things she loves, from snoozing dogs to chocolate eclairs. It is good to be reminded that there is a world out there beyond grief and suffering, and beyond constraining notions of virtue and obligation – an anarchic world of cream cakes and dreams and sun.

Loves it, Johanna would have said, quoting Paris Hilton's cooking show (Johanna loved camp TV).

When she was told she had three months to live, a well-meaning oncologist suggested she might feel her cancer was *unfair*. 'You might feel why me, why is this happening to me,' he carried on, not quite reading her expression on the screen.

'Well, why not me?' Johanna asked, laughing.

Why not me. Isn't that wonderful? ■

Sigrid Rausing

LETTERS FROM UKRAINE

Lindsey Hilsum

I reported for Channel 4 News *from Ukraine during the first weeks of the invasion. These are expanded versions of letters that I wrote home.*

Hotel InterContinental, Kyiv
Monday, 14 March 2022

My team and I are staying at the InterCon in Kyiv, reporting on the war day by day. It's hard to plan, because things change by the hour. Central Kyiv is not that dangerous for now. The shelling remains on the outskirts, but every day the Russians get a bit closer.

At the railway station we saw little knots of women wheeling small cheap suitcases, accompanied by children who didn't know whether to be fearful or excited, carrying multicoloured backpacks hung with stuffed toys. Men aren't allowed to leave the country, and most would rather stay and fight (from what I can tell), so those leaving are nearly all women. We met a grandmother, mother and daughter who left northern Kyiv because the house next door to theirs took a direct hit this morning. A young woman in a purple woolly hat, jiggling a plump, smiling six-month-old baby, told me she had left not only her husband but also her mother in Chernihiv. Her mother refuses to leave her dad, but the young woman's priority is getting the baby out. And the there was the family, including granny in a wheelchair, whos village to the north-east of Kyiv had been occupied by the Russians The mother, Olena, told me, 'They all had machine guns, and we weren't allowed to go anywhere.' A few days ago, the Russians finally agreed a 'green corridor', an evacuation route, but then they shot civilians as they tried to leave. 'Some survived but others were wounded or killed. Many bodies were just left there. Any corpses that could be taken away were buried in gardens and in the park.'

I've been here nearly four weeks, and I was also here for ten days in January. The last time I spent so much time in Ukraine was back in 2014, when the Russians annexed Crimea and split off the eastern Donbas region from the rest of the country, creating the Donetsk and Luhansk 'People's Republics' – separatist statelets that remain under Russian control. The war has sputtered on ever since but the lines have scarcely moved. It's estimated that 14,000 people – Ukrainian soldiers, civilians and separatists – have been killed from the start of that conflict until now. When we ask Ukrainians about the war now, they usually say, 'But we've been at war for eight years already.' Back in 2014, when the Russians first appeared in the Crimean capital, Simferopol, I happened to be at the airport. Famously, they wore no insignia on their Spetsnaz uniforms, hence the moniker 'little green men'. I went up to a group of them and stuck a microphone in their faces, asking, in my one sentence of Russian, '*Voi Russki soldat?*' – 'Are you a Russian soldier?' 'No comment,' they growled in English. If doubt was contrived then, it's non-existent now. Putin denied he was planning to invade Ukraine, but from late last year we could see on satellite pictures how he was amassing forces on the borders. As Western intelligence agencies started to brief journalists that he was planning a full-scale invasion, I found it hard to believe. But they were absolutely right.

On the first day of the invasion I was in Kramatorsk, an unlovely town in the east near the area Russia has controlled since 2014. I was with my team: camera operator Philippa, producer Simon, local producer Maksym and Eduard 'Red Shoes', our taciturn driver. In the early hours of the morning we were woken by loud explosions, which turned out to be artillery attacks on military targets around the town. As we were staying in a small hotel inside an apartment block, we decided to drive through the darkness to a larger hotel where many other journalists were staying, which we thought might be safer. It was chaos. Some journalists were in the basement bomb shelter, convinced they were about to die. Others were broadcasting live from the porch. Nothing was going bang anywhere near. The press corps was overexcited. 'I have never been in a war before!' a Mexican journalist exclaimed. 'What shall I do?' I suggested that keeping calm was probably a good start. 'Maybe at your age you don't care about saving your life!' a French journalist shouted at me as he hurtled past, on his way down to the shelter. I don't think it was a compliment.

We decided to head west to Dnipro, given that the Russians were so near to Kramatorsk. It would have been easy for them to march in and take the town (in the event, they didn't). People were beginning to line up at cashpoints, and as we drove out of town queues were forming at petrol stations. Luckily, we'd had the forethought to fill up the day before. We stopped to interview people. 'I'm going to fill my tank and go fishing,' said one old man, with admirable sangfroid.

Dnipro, on the banks of the Dnipro River, was not initially a target although it has been hit several times since. We stayed at the Menorah Hotel in the Jewish Centre. As Putin claimed to be 'de-Nazifying' Ukraine, we thought it would be a bit of an own goal if it was hit by a rocket. They also served very good cheesecake. The only disadvantage was that to test the air-raid alarm system, which involved VERY LOUD announcements through speakers in every room, they played 'Guantanamera' on a loop. At my behest, Simon took a screwdriver to detach the wires, and then replaced the speaker cover in each of our rooms. At least we would be able to sleep. There was really no point in going to a bomb shelter just because the siren sounded. Our hotel was unlikely to be a target. And – as every soldier and every journalist who has ever covered a war knows – sleeping and eating are the most important things. If you don't sleep and eat, you get grumpy and make bad decisions.

Dnipro was getting ready for war. In a central square, next to a model spaceship, a small army of young women was making Molotov cocktails to throw at Russian tanks. One contingent was tearing up polystyrene foam to make the cocktails stick better to their targets, a chemistry lesson best not repeated at home. I got chatting to a young man who ran a music studio. 'We heard stories of our grandfathers who had to fight Nazism,' he said. 'Now we are like our grandfathers.' I asked if his generation was up to it. 'Yes,' he replied. 'If Putin thought he can beat us he is mistaken big time.' He was rather impressed by the British prime minister, because the UK had provided the Ukrainians with anti-tank weapons. 'Boris is a strange man but we thank him,' he said. The Queen, incidentally, is also popular. On at least one occasion it was remarked that I look like her. Again, I am not sure this was a compliment – I am after all more than thirty years her junior. I never understand what Maksym, our local producer, tells Ukrainian soldiers on checkpoints to persuade them to let us through, but I gather that the phrases 'Very famous journalist', 'Knows the Queen' and 'Saw Gaddafi's body with her own eyes' have all been uttered. I just smile and wave.

We drove to the Moldovan border, where Philippa and Simon were due to leave us. Soren, the cameraman I normally work with, another producer, Rob, and a paramedic, Dom, were there to swap in. With Maksym and Eduard 'Red Shoes' we made a good team. No one who panicked. No one trying to be a hero. Everyone wanting to get the story. We continued our tour of places that might, or might not, become a front line. Odesa was beautiful and sad, the famous rococo opera house partially obscured by fortified barricades. Someone had spray-painted over the street names and wrapped the signposts in black plastic bags, like rural England circa 1942, with all those cunning plans to foil the Germans. I suspected, however, that the Russians had Google Maps. At the yacht club, we filmed an assembly line filling sandbags while the radio played 'You're Beautiful'. Volunteers had gathered at a food court to receive and pack supplies for the troops – clothes, food, medicines. A poster showed what should have been happening there that weekend: the Odesa Jazz and Oysters Festival.

The neighbouring Black Sea port of Mykolaiv was shelled before we arrived. We stood on the riverbank and watched black smoke rising from one of the buildings that had been hit. A food warehouse – the Russians appear to be targeting civilian food stores. A few days later we saw a similar scene north of Kyiv. All the hotels were closed, and we slept on mattresses on the floor of a makeshift police station, sharing a bathroom with fifty or so Territorial Defence volunteers who were stretched out in the corridors, fully clad in their uniforms and boots, rifles at their side. Luxury it was not, but they were incredibly kind and hospitable. On International Women's Day, 8 March, Ukrainian men usually give women flowers. A rather grizzled volunteer came into our room and thrust a paper cone into my hands. 'We have no tulips,' he apologised, and when I looked I found a pot of honey inside. They also fed us soup, cheese and sausages, so we didn't have to resort to the normal wartime journalists' diet of whisky and Pringles. (But we consumed those too.)

The governor of Mykolaiv, Vitaliy Kim, is something of a President Zelenskiy lookalike. Both are in their early forties, and have adopted military garb. We interviewed Kim outside the municipal office.[1] He's quite funny. The Russian flag sports an eagle, while the Ukrainian flag has a trident. 'No country with a chicken as an emblem should invade one with a fork,' he likes to say. He gave us a military escort to see the damage wreaked by the previous day's bombing. We watched soldiers digging through the wreckage of their barracks, which had been hit by artillery: eight men had been killed and at least eight more were missing, maybe buried in the rubble. At a neighbourhood on the outskirts of town, we came across four teenagers with piercings and blue/pink/green hair; like most people their age, they had defined themselves through personal rebellion, but in a few hours their whole lives had changed. The previous night their homes had been destroyed. I asked Violetta, who was seventeen, what she would say to Putin if

---

[1] Two weeks later, the building was hit by a rocket. At least thirty-five people were killed, but Governor Kim wasn't there. He said he was late that morning as he had overslept.

she saw him. 'I would ask him, why are you doing this? Does this look like a rescue operation to you? People are dying, people have nowhere to live. Does this look like salvation to you?'

Because that's the biggest lie – that Putin has invaded to save Ukrainians from their own government. He says he's 'de-Nazifying' a country which elected a Jew as president. He's 'saving' Russian speakers, who are perfectly safe in an independent Ukraine. But for how much longer will they speak Russian? 'Russian is now the language of my enemy even though it's what my family speaks,' one young woman told me. 'I will never speak it again.' Maksym tells me that some people we interview insist on speaking Ukrainian, even though they would be more comfortable in Russian. Putin says Ukraine isn't a real country, just 'Little Russia', a part of the Russian empire. His vision reaches back to tsarist times. For Ukrainians this is an anti-colonial struggle, and that's one reason there's such an upswell of patriotic fervour. The spirit of resistance is leavened by humour. In the Kyiv Children's Hospital, I met thirteen-year-old Vova, who was badly injured when the car his family was travelling in was hit. He has tubes coming out of his nose and can't speak because his jaw has been wired shut, so he writes on a pad. He wrote down what he wanted: 'Phone. Toy car. Puzzle.' Then what he was thinking: 'Putin is a dick!'

I have been so busy reporting, I don't think I have got my head round the import of what is going on. Yet I do know that this war has a significance beyond most stories I've reported. The two seminal historic events in my lifetime as a journalist have been the fall of the Berlin Wall and 9/11. Most of my reporting has been about what flowed from the latter: Afghanistan, Iraq, Syria. But this is a third seismic event. At the time of writing we are in the perilous moment of not knowing if the war will widen, and bring NATO into direct conflict with Russia. Whether Ukraine will survive. Whether Putin will survive. Anything could happen.

Yesterday, we were shelled a little on the outskirts of Irpin, a commuter town north-west of Kyiv. Arguably I am too old for this. I run like a penguin. Two soldiers obviously thought I looked like their granny and tried to carry me, so I had to fight them off while under fire. It was more humiliating than dangerous – the shells all fell quite a distance away. I'm not reckless, but I wouldn't be anywhere else right now. At some point we may have to pull out – if they besiege Kyiv there will be shortages and I'm not going to eat roasted rat. For the moment, the road south remains clear and (amazingly) there are still trains to Lviv. I want to hang on for a bit, as there is much more to report. Then I'll come home and try to make sense of it all.

Hotel Axelhof, Dnipro
Friday, 18 March 2022

Kyiv calmed down a bit, so we headed east, back to Dnipro. The city remains mostly calm, and we wanted to find people fleeing Mariupol. Last time I was here, the hotel tried to force us into the bunker whenever the siren sounded, even though it was nearly always a false alarm. Now no one bothers. When the siren wails, they close the shops. No one hides or looks for a cellar. People queue on the pavement, waiting for it to be over.

We're all sobered by the loss of our colleagues. On Sunday an American film-maker, Brent Renaud, was killed in Irpin, the town north-west of Kyiv, near where we were shelled the other day. Then the Fox News team went missing in Bucha, the adjacent town. Seems their car came under artillery fire. Their correspondent Benjamin Hall is in hospital; I'm told that his leg was amputated. The local producer, Oleksandra Kuvshynova, a young woman of only twenty-four, was killed, as was the cameraman, Pierre Zakrzewski. Pierre was a lanky, humorous fellow with a Borat moustache and curly hair, which went grey over the time I knew him. We were embedded with the same US marine unit during the battle for Fallujah in 2004. He was Irish, with a Polish surname, and a real traveller. Everyone knew him because you saw him everywhere. The story is that the Russians killed the journalists, and that may be true. Or maybe with Brent it was jumpy

Ukrainian checkpoint guys. We'll probably never know. What we do know is that it's too dangerous to report from the outskirts of Kyiv.

I am amazed at how many journalists are in Ukraine – a couple of WhatsApp and Signal groups I'm on have exceeded their limit, one is up to 3,000 members. It's a Wizz Air war: you can fly on a budget airline to Poland, then hitch a ride in or take the train. No visas, very few restrictions. That means lots of inexperienced freelancers have shown up, but they're not necessarily the ones who get killed – Pierre was very experienced. It's not like Syria, where it was hard to get a visa to report from the government side, and then you had to negotiate with minders to film anything at all. Going in on the rebel side became too dangerous for most of us, after Marie Colvin and Rémi Ochlik were killed by artillery fire in 2012, and James Foley was kidnapped and murdered by ISIS. This is more like Bosnia, which was also accessible. The InterCon in Kyiv is full of journalists swapping notes at breakfast before heading out into the city or beyond. It's a sad reflection on my social life that much of it is here – half the people I've ever known are in Ukraine. The hotel staff were amazingly kind and adaptable, and many of them stayed in the hotel so they didn't have to go home after curfew at 10 p.m. They served an extra meal between 4 p.m. and 7 p.m. so we could all eat, and they even managed to keep doing laundry.

The Ukrainians have been remarkably successful in holding off the Russian advance. Back in 2014, in Crimea, I remember watching Ukrainian units being forced to surrender to the Russians because they had neither the weapons nor the men to resist. They marched out of their bases in formation, carrying their flag, trying to maintain pride despite being defeated without a fight. But they have spent the last eight years training with modern weapons provided by NATO countries, and have become a far more nimble force. The Russians, by contrast, seem to have overestimated their chances of achieving a rapid victory. But the war could go on a long time. The Ukrainian authorities are on the whole helpful to journalists – they can see that in a David and Goliath struggle, sympathy is with David. Every government and army has something to hide, but the Ukrainians have less than most: they were invaded, and this is a democracy, so there's an understanding of who we are and enthusiasm for what we do. But soon Ukraine will slip down the running order of TV bulletins. We will start looking for less obvious stories. Some Ukrainian soldiers somewhere will be found to have abused or shot Russian prisoners. More will be written about the Azov brigade, which is defending Mariupol, and was originally a neo-Nazi force. It's been absorbed into the Ukrainian military and now incorporates different political views, but still – there are always questions to ask. Things will begin to look less clear-cut, murkier. And then the Ukrainian authorities may get angry with the international press, introduce censorship and start to restrict us.

Every night in the early hours, the Russians shell residential areas of Kyiv. On Tuesday they hit at least three neighbourhoods. You will be familiar with the footage: flames licking out from blown windows, firefighters wielding hoses, black smoke billowing. On one block, after the flames were extinguished, we saw people sorting through the wreckage – a woman shaking a red carpet covered in debris from the balcony, a guy pulling out broken furniture from the ruins, another chucking out huge pieces of rubble with his bare hands. A great tangle of metal rods, crumbled concrete, splintered wood – all the ruptured interstices of a modern apartment block – spilled out. We drove to another block where the firefighters were still in action; grey smoke was billowing from the top half of the building, while sooty water from the hosepipes fell from the balconies in a thin, dark rain. The mayor of Kyiv, former heavyweight champion Vitali Klitschko, had turned up to survey the scene. Standing six foot six, his bulk increased by a blue padded jacket and a khaki flak jacket, he's an impressive figure. Maksym took a picture of our interview, in which I am between him and Soren, my six-foot-five Danish cameraman. I look like a tiny, delicate insect peering up at a giant. Klitschko is a popular mayor, now more than ever. I asked what his advice was to the people of Kyiv. 'Keep together. Stay strong,' he said. 'Defend our houses. Defend our families, children, future, country, principles, values.'

I also met Olha, who's twenty-seven, works for a British marketing company and lives in an adjacent block. She and her husband were asleep on the couch, which shook when the shell impacted. They spent the rest of the night sleeping on the floor, clinging tight to each other, expecting the next shell to hit them. 'It's always fifty–fifty,' she said. 'Either you get hit or not.' She spoke precise English and seemed remarkably composed, until I asked how she felt about Russia, when her voice hardened. 'Now I understand that we will never be friends again with anybody of Russian people,' she said. I asked the typical journalist's question about whether she distinguished between the Russian government and the people. She did not.

I keep thinking about how a country can be transformed so quickly. Back in January, we filmed at the Kharkiv Dog Show – the Ukrainian equivalent of Crufts. People were a bit anxious, but I don't think anyone believed the war would really happen as they paraded their hounds around the ring. Now Kharkiv is under constant artillery attack; the buildings around the central square where we wandered have been destroyed. Slawa, the local producer we worked with then, volunteered to rejoin the army and was injured while fighting north-west of Kyiv. 'It was shell splinter. Hit me in the back below the armour,' he WhatsApped me. Hope was tinged with realism. 'We will break their spine. But the cost might be very high.'

In the first days of the war, we filmed a checkpoint being built just south of Dnipro: a digger was excavating trenches, some guys were lugging sandbags into place while others did target practice. Now all the roads are studded with checkpoints, iron girders turned into tank traps that look like giant versions of the metal jacks we used to play with as kids, throwing them in the air and catching them on the backs of our hands.

We must have travelled thousands of miles, along endless avenues of trees, great balls of mistletoe hanging from their leafless branches, spread, it's said, by rooks. In the first week or so, as we drove towards the war, everyone else was driving away – we passed long queues of cars heading to the borders. Ukrainian highway service stations remain stocked with biscuits, energy drinks, gadgets, soft toys and games to keep children entertained on a journey. The freezers are full of ice cream, as if the families packed into cars should be going on a summer holiday, not into exile.

New posters have gone up everywhere. A day after the war began, Russian marines tried to force a group of Ukrainian border guards on Snake Island in the Black Sea to surrender. The radio transmissions were recorded and broadcast: 'I am a Russian warship. I am a Russian warship. Put down arms immediately to avoid bloodshed and unjustified deaths.' To which the Ukrainians replied, 'Russian warship, go fuck yourself!' It's become a meme. Everywhere we go, we see billboards plastered with variations on those words: 'Russian warship/train/fighter jet, go fuck yourself!' There's even one depicting the Kremlin as a ship going down in a sea of blood.[2]

Hotel Opera Centre, Lviv
Thursday, 24 March 2022

We've been gathering testimonies of the people fleeing Mariupol. It's the worst horror of this war so far, if I can create a hierarchy of horror. I think Mariupol will go down in history like Guernica, or Leningrad or Aleppo – places that have been besieged and bombarded with no regard for civilian life. Water, electricity, phones and internet have all been cut off, and both artillery fire and aerial bombing are relentless. The Russians are determined to seize control of Mariupol because it would enable them to link Crimea and the two 'People's Republics' of Donetsk and Luhansk, which they have occupied since 2014. It would give them a contiguous swathe of Ukraine.

---

[2] On 29 March, the Ukrainian government announced that the Snake Island soldiers had been freed in a prisoner exchange, and that Roman Hrybov, who had told the Russians where to go, had been awarded a medal.

We went to the car park of a DIY store on the southern side of Zaporizhzhia, which the local authorities had established as a place to register and help those fleeing Mariupol, and watched a caravan of bedraggled cars arrive. Most sported torn white cloths to show they were civilian, not military, vehicles, and had a sign with the word дитя, meaning 'child' in Russian, pasted on the windows. Many vehicles were held together with bubble wrap and tape, their windscreens shattered by shrapnel. One guy, Vlad, had driven for two days in a smashed-up car while towing his friend, whose car was even more damaged. He had managed to preserve the footage he had shot on his phone of Russian armoured vehicles with the characteristic Z on the side, the Russian symbol. He'd also filmed his own apartment, littered with broken glass from the shell that had taken out the floor below. Hard to understand how he, or it, had survived. Such footage is rare; most people we met told us that the Russians and Chechens on the multiple roadblocks they passed through on the way out had forced them to wipe their phones. The Russians know all about evidence of war crimes.

I felt a bit worried about sticking a microphone in people's faces – all these years as a reporter and I still have that British reserve and concern about being intrusive. (Except with Russian soldiers pretending they're not Russian soldiers.) But people were desperate to speak. Most had been on the road for at least two days, after weeks of relentless bombardment. This was the first time they felt safe, and they just wanted to talk about what they had endured and the horror they had survived. One woman, Maria, spoke English. She described how her two children – Igor, aged thirteen, and Eva-Elisabeta, aged fifteen – had been near the Mariupol Drama Theatre when it was bombed on 16 March. Everything turned into slow motion after she heard the explosion, and she found herself running through grit and flying stones, yelling out her children's names. She could scarcely believe it when she finally heard their voices – in that moment she had been convinced they were dead. We still don't know how many people were killed in that attack. Several hundred women and children are thought to have been in the basement, but it's not clear if they survived or were buried in the rubble.[3]

Igor and Eva-Elisabeta were in the back of a white van, huddled with blankets and cushions, making sure their cat, peeping out of a small backpack, did not escape. The neighbour's son was also there, and a large dog who growled when we tried to film too close. I liked that; I felt he was trying to protect them. Maria's mother, who had cooked for the family throughout the siege, sometimes on a log fire in the street, was in the front seat. They were heading for Germany. The kids seemed relieved and happy to be out of Mariupol. No tears. Will they be traumatised? Possibly. But they have a strong and determined mother which must surely help. And one thing I've learnt from covering wars for three decades is that people are amazingly resilient, and often live productive and happy lives after enduring appalling suffering.

So many stories . . . all horrific. I have no doubt that these people are victims of, and witnesses to, war crimes. I fear we will hear many more such stories before this conflict is over. Maria said something that has stuck with me. 'I heard that our president gave our city the name of hero. But it's not true,' she said. 'People are horrible right now. The war shows your real face.' People were stealing food from supermarkets and not sharing it with their neighbours. They weren't helping each other – she had spent days trying to find a lift out but most people refused. It made me think of the myths war (and war propaganda) create. The British like to talk of the Blitz spirit, and forget the stealing and other crimes that went on in London under German bombs during the blackout. In Ukraine, everything is hung in the national colours – bright blue and sunshine yellow. There's a spirit of defiance and unity, fomented partly by President Zelenskiy, whose refusal to leave Kyiv and nightly broadcasts have undoubtedly inspired the nation. One young man on a checkpoint told me it was Zelenskiy's

---

[3] At the time of writing, the Ukrainian authorities have put the death toll at 300, but no accurate count can be made as the Russians occupy the area.

example that made him determined to stay and fight. But when it gets to the kind of pressure the people of Mariupol are under, it's hard to live up to a patriotic ideal. Life becomes a matter of simple survival, and about saving your close family. War brings out the best and the worst in people.

Maria also said that some people in Mariupol were welcoming the Russians, because they believed Russian propaganda that the Ukrainian government was going to stop them speaking Russian. 'I'm sorry to say but it's bullshit – we all speak Russian and nobody ever denied us to speak like this,' she said. Back in 2014, I met people in Crimea and the Donbas who looked east to Russia rather than west to Europe. In the subsequent eight years, while those areas stagnated, and sporadic clashes continued to take lives, many changed their minds. Young people moved to other parts of Ukraine, and now the 'People's Republics' are largely inhabited by the elderly, surviving off their old Soviet pensions. But a nation is never entirely united, and nowhere is that more true than Ukraine with its fractured and contested history. I doubt Maria will see her Russophile neighbours again. She didn't think she would ever return. Satellite pictures show that Mariupol is utterly destroyed. The Ukrainian army is battling to retain control of ruins. The Russians will inevitably take the city because they need the territory, but as one woman said to me, 'Mariupol no longer exists.' I thought of Tacitus writing in the voice of Calgacus, describing the Roman conquest of Britain, 'They created a desolation and called it peace.'

If staying in Mariupol is unbearably dangerous, leaving may be equally so. We spent Tuesday at the children's hospital in Zaporizhzhia, where they're treating kids who were shot on the way out. I already mentioned the Russian checkpoints, many manned by Chechens, where they wipe people's phones and demand to see their documents. Sometimes they then open fire. We found several children who were injured, including eleven-year-old Milena, who left with her family on 16 March. The doctor says she'll survive, although she looked pretty sick with tubes everywhere, gasping for breath, her bed protected from potential shelling by sandbags piled up against the window. Her mother, Olena, said their car had become separated from the rest of the convoy and went through the checkpoint last. She recognised the soldiers as Chechens because of their appearance and their broken Russian. They pointed guns at the vehicle but let them through. Then they fired. The car stopped, and the Chechens came rushing up, denying that they had been the ones to shoot. Olena challenged them – who else could it be? There was no one else around. When they saw they had injured the little girl, they took the family to a hospital nearby. Later they helped them contact the Red Cross to take them to Zaporizhzhia.

Such is the insanity of war. First you shoot up a car, injuring a child. Then you try to save her. What was going through their heads? It made me think of Rwanda back in 1994, when I interviewed Hutus who had hidden a Tutsi neighbour in their ceiling, but killed many others. When accused of murdering their neighbours, the defence wasn't 'I didn't do it', but 'OK, I killed some Tutsis. But I saved others.'

This letter is more grim than the last – I guess that's how the war has gone. It's not about the danger we're in – apart from that one incident outside Irpin, we haven't been near the front line, unlike other journalists who have been accompanying Ukrainian forces. The Russians have failed to take Kyiv or Kharkiv and are being pushed back. They're not winning the war as Putin thought they would, and the Ukrainian military – so much more flexible and reactive – is doing incredibly well in defending their country. In the years to come, there will be much to discover about why the Russians thought they would have an easy victory, whether Putin's generals and intelligence operatives told him the truth, and the roots of Russian imperial overreach. But while I'm here now, what interests me most is the stories of civilians who never wanted to be near a front line.

One positive aspect of modern reporting is that I can keep in touch with people I have interviewed by WhatsApp or Signal, so I message Maria and Olha from time to time. Maria has crossed the border to Poland now – her children will probably grow up in Germany. Olha and her husband, for the moment, remain in Kyiv. She says they could leave, but they'd like to stay if they can, and help the old people who have no means of getting out. Slawa, our former producer, is recovering in hospital – he doesn't know when he'll be well enough to fight again. Vova, the injured boy who wrote on his pad 'Putin is a dick!' has become famous – several other journalists have filmed him. He looks like he's improving physically, but I wonder how he's feeling inside. When we met him, his mother hadn't let him know that the explosion that injured him killed his father. She must have told him by now.

I'm writing this on my last day in Ukraine, five weeks after I arrived. We drove west from Dnipro to Khmelnytskyi, named after a sixteenth-century Ukrainian military commander who led an uprising against Polish rule, but ended up doing a deal with the Russians that placed part of Ukraine under their control. I took a picture of a massive statue depicting him – of course – on a giant horse. (Inevitably, the old woman sweeping below suspected I was a Russian saboteur and turned me over to the local Territorial Defence volunteers. Luckily, once they realised I was a journalist, they were very understanding and chatty, curious to know what I had seen further east.) Geography condemns Ukraine to war, positioned as it is between the Russian and the historic European empires. Will Zelenskiy, like Khmelnytsky, have to agree to Russia retaining control over part of Ukrainian territory? If he does, would the Ukrainian people still see him as a hero, or would he suddenly become a traitor? The obvious sacrifice would be an expanded Donbas plus some territory in the south that links to Crimea, but it's hard to imagine Ukrainians agreeing to that. How would you feel if you had defended your country as Ukrainians have, only to see part of it given away? And yet, how else can any kind of peace deal be agreed?

Onward from Khmelnytskyi to Lviv. In the time I've been here, winter has turned to spring. The snow has largely melted and the vast, flat, deep-brown fields are tinged with green. Ukraine is one of the world's biggest exporters of wheat and sunflower seeds. If they can't fertilise the crops now, or can't export their produce, the price of bread and sunflower oil will shoot up all over the world, adding to the global cost-of-living crisis caused by a rise in gas prices. This war is a stone thrown into a pond – the ripples will spread. Maybe the increase in food and gas prices will trigger riots and revolution somewhere that has nothing to do with Russia or Ukraine, in Africa or the Middle East. Wars always have consequences that no one intends or foresees.

Lviv seems like another country: the shops are open, people are out on the streets, going to cafes and restaurants. I feel as if we have gone through a portal into another reality. Tomorrow we'll cross the border to Poland and fly home. I feel bad about leaving, but I am also very tired. I need to stop and think. And then I'll return.

Hotel Axelhof, Dnipro
Sunday, 1 May 2022

I've been back for nearly two weeks, and wish I'd returned sooner. It's not as if I stopped thinking about Ukraine while I was at home – this isn't a story you can leave behind. While I was away Russian forces retreated from the towns north-west of Kyiv, revealing a trail of horror behind them, as if their trucks pulled back the cover over a pit as they departed. Along with the destruction of Mariupol, the atrocities at Bucha will go down as the signature war crimes of this conflict: people with their hands tied behind their backs shot in the head, women raped, children's bodies lying in the street. In one incident, Russian soldiers gave rations to people huddled in a basement – and then threw in a grenade.

The jocular patriotism among Ukrainians that I saw on my last trip has been replaced by grim fury. People I meet don't care how long this war takes, nor even how much suffering they individually endure – they just need to win. And they believe that if they get enough new weapons, they will do. The Russians were forced to abandon a lot of armour when they retreated from the Kyiv area, and lost maybe 15,000 men; now they're regrouping with the aim of taking more territory in the east and joining that to the area they control in the south. The Ukrainians certainly have the advantage when it comes to morale and determination, but this is an artillery war, and the Russians don't seem to be running out of shells.

In Moscow and in Western capitals it's all about arrows and shaded areas on a map. Here it's about old people being shelled in villages, and young people fighting in trenches. We're moving around the east, but as yet not in the area where fighting is most intense. As we drive along the roads we see long columns of trucks carrying soldiers to the front line. Most of the conflicts I've covered in the past have been civil wars, guerrilla struggles or Western interventions against scrappy bands of fighters. This feels more like the First or Second World War – conventional armies pitted against each other across the black earth, now turning green with the spring rains.

In the village of Kamianske, the last Ukrainian-held village south of Zaporizhzhia, we found a young couple called Lina and Yakiv. Although they'd left for the city after their house was destroyed in early March, they drove their battered old car back to bring supplies to elderly neighbours who had remained behind. We went to look at their destroyed home. Lina's father, Leonid, had been killed while standing in the kitchen as a rocket struck. The moment of impact had been frozen in time. The roof was shattered and debris was scattered everywhere, but a frying pan lay untouched on the hob. There was a jar of pickles on the countertop, and a photograph of Leonid's wedding to Lina's mother still hung on the wall. Outside, the apple blossom was in full, delicate, white flower, and the tulips bloomed scarlet like poppies in the battlefields of the Somme. I tried to imagine Lina's parents feeding the chickens and admiring their garden last spring. They could never have imagined what was about to happen.

We drove on to Zelenodolsk, where people from the southern city of Kherson and its surrounding villages are arriving. Kherson was the first city to be seized by the Russians back at the beginning of the war. I remember seeing lots of videos on Twitter showing Ukrainians protesting with their blue-and-yellow flags in the main square. Since then, protesters have been arrested or beaten, and the Russians have consolidated control, raising the Russian tricolour over the municipal building and installing a puppet leadership. They don't seem to have committed the same atrocities as in Bucha, or at least not on the same scale. Still, every day people arrive in Zelenodolsk, usually by foot or on bicycles as cars are mostly turned back at the Russian checkpoints. The local Ukrainian authorities have gathered these bikes and store them in a huge shed – thousands are piled up, plus a few buggies and the occasional wheelchair.

We were chatting to some women who had arrived that morning when an old man shambled up, sat down on a chair and ate a yogurt that volunteers had provided. His hands were shaking. He removed his black woolly hat to show us his head, which was entirely bandaged, the ragged ends tied beneath his chin. His name was Oleksander. He lived in a village occupied by the Russians. A few days earlier, three drunken Russian soldiers had barged into his neighbour's house demanding food and vodka. When he remonstrated with them, they set about him with an axe handle. His face was bruised, and his ribs were broken. He said he felt sick all the time. He seemed utterly bewildered.

How much longer will this go on? How many more Leonids and Oleksanders? The US and other NATO countries are sending in huge amounts of weapons. They clearly think they can help the Ukrainians not just to resist but also to defeat the Russians, incapacitating the Russian military for a generation. Ukrainian officers I meet thank me for the anti-tank weapons the British are sending. No one is saying they want to surrender, or that they fear Putin will be provoked into a nuclear strike, or that they are worried the munitions will only prolong the war – all the arguments being made against further Western involvement that you hear outside the country. Yet, despite the weakness of the Russian military revealed by their defeat around Kyiv, they seem to have an endless supply of artillery, and may continue to fight even if neither side is gaining ground. I fear how much destruction and death will have been wrought by the time the tulips bloom next spring. ∎

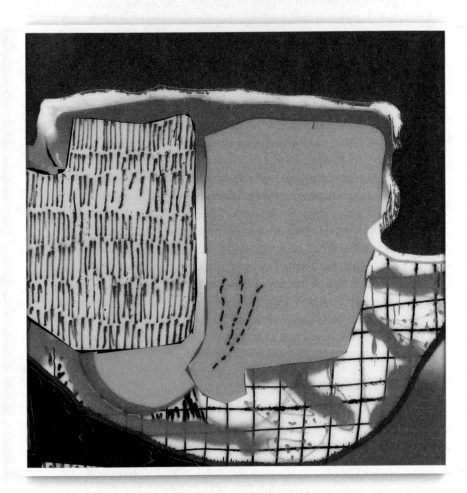

TIM GARWOOD
Polyester Temple, 2016

I AM THE WORD FOR GOD AND BOY

Aidan Cottrell-Boyce

The night before the wedding we're in a cafe on the corner of Elgin Avenue for dinner. Caroline takes out a piece of folded-up paper and smooths it out on the tabletop. She isn't going to make a speech at the wedding, but she has written one anyway. In a parallel universe, she tells me, this is what she would say.

'I'm just going to read it for you instead,' she says.

Outside the sky is black and clear, and you can see the actual universe in the sky, and the lighting in the cafe is warm like a bead of amber. We are sitting in a cafe, on planet Earth, on the night before our wedding day.

'Thank you especially to Pol,' Caroline says, 'for allowing me to dote on him.'

She folds up the piece of paper and puts it in the pocket of her overcoat, which is hanging on the back of her chair. She puts her hands on the table and interlaces her fingers and smiles. I tell her that she should make the speech at the wedding. She shakes her head.

'All those people,' she says. The radio in the cafe is playing 'Sailing' by Rod Stewart.

'Don't forget to call the sandwiches guy,' she says.

She leaves and goes back to her parents' house in Queen's Park where her wedding dress is hanging on the back of her childhood bedroom door. I tell her that I am going back to my mother's house but instead I walk up to the Heath, to the men's pond. I jump over the gate and I walk down the path, past the toilets and the locked door to the changing area, past the lifeguard's hut. The water is as black as ink. I clamber down the banks and slip off my trousers and boxers and I climb down the ladder into the water. The skin of the water is covered in small insects.

On the banks is a bald man, watching me. I plunge my hands down into the water and then I plunge my head down into the water, trying not to think about breathing. It's fucking cold. At the bottom of the pond there is a glimmer of light, which gets bigger and bigger as I swim towards it.

There is a church glowing with blue sunlight. Everyone is standing in the narthex. Light pours through the stained-glass windows, pink and blue. A boy wearing blue and a girl wearing pink, who I don't recognise, are running down the side aisle and their small smart shoes are clack-clacking on the loose parts of the herringbone floor. It's a Victorian church, neo-Gothic, but the decor is beige and pastel. There are twentieth-century Stations of the Cross hanging on the walls and twentieth-century stained-glass windows. My sister Caoimhe is there, and Father Edward. Caoimhe's current boyfriend is there too. I can see Caroline's parents huddled together in a corner, trying not to make eye contact with any of my relatives. There are a few other people I don't know: Caroline's colleagues from school. Caroline's American cousin is there with her husband. Father Edward is still wearing his civilian clothes: a pair of canvas slacks and a sky-blue, short-sleeved shirt. The only person wearing a hat is Caroline's American cousin. Caoimhe is wearing a tartan shirt and a pair of high-waisted jeans. Caoimhe sidles up to me and she nudges me.

'Nice suit,' she says.

'Thanks,' I say.
'Where's Mum?' she says.
'She went to the bathroom,' I say.
'Where's Caroline?' she says.
I shrug.
'Morning sickness?' she says.
I look at her.
'She isn't pregnant,' I say.
And Caoimhe grins.

Now I'm standing at the front of the church, before the altar. The altar linen is rough to the touch from being laundered and ironed too many times. The surface of the altar mantle rustles inaudibly against the ridges of my fingertip. My mother used to launder and iron these cloths. Sometimes Caoimhe or our neighbour, Mrs Evans, would help her. They would stand at the ironing board in the living room on Quex Road, ironing. The next day I would see the same cloths that had been in our living room on the altar. A breeze from the half-open door at the side of the church moving them, slightly. The incongruity would make my head swim.

The congregation rises. I know that Caroline is here now. I don't look back. Instead I pray silently. Please allow me the strength not to desire to convince her that she is shrewish, I pray. Please allow me the strength not to desire to convince her that she is shrewish.

Later on, years later, Caroline will say that I looked so nervous, that I didn't even look her in the eye, and I will ask well what is the implication of that and she will just say:
'No implication. You just didn't look me in the eye.'

At the back of the church a baby is lowing. I can hear a low hum coming from inside the priest's chest. The battery pack for his microphone, hidden inside his alb, humming. His eyes are locked on Caroline's.

She is trying to remember the words. I can feel everybody looking at us: her American cousin and her American cousin's husband.

'*You* remember,' her American cousin kept saying, over and over, prodding her husband, when we had lunch with them last week. 'You *do* remember.'

'*Allow* him man,' Caoimhe will say to me later, after she has been forced to sit next to him for hours at the wedding breakfast. She is scornful of the shy. 'Simply *allow*.'
     'Since when do you talk like that?' I will say.
     '*Allow* him,' Caoimhe will say, again.

I should be taking all of this in. I should be listening to the words. I pinch the outside of my thigh through the pocket of my wedding trousers with my finger and my thumb.
     'I, Pol,' says the priest.
     'I, Pol,' I reply.

My mother thought that it was contrarian of my father to want to call me Polonius. She agreed only on the condition that they would abbreviate it to Pol. But from the day that I was born, my mother started calling me Polly. When she first met my mother, Caroline took to calling me Polly too: firstly to mimic my mother and later on out of habit. They were the only two people in the world who called me that.

I still don't know why he wanted to name me Polonius. I think he maybe just thought that it would help him to feel sorry for me. He found it difficult to feel sorry for people.

He was teaching English at a gymnasium in Frankfurt and finishing his doctoral studies when I was born. He was a Shakespeare man, an Anglophile. When he first met my mother he assumed that she was English. They were already in love before she told him that she wasn't. She was Irish and shy and spry and younger than he was by a good ten years. She was studying at the art school, the Städelschule. She was studying to be a painter.

I find it hard to separate my own memories *of* him from anecdotes *about* him. Like trying to separate the sight that you have out of one eye from the sight that you have out of the other. He was a pissed-off man, my mother would say, later. He had little round spectacles that he wore even when he was nude. He went swimming in the sea, nude, even when there were other people around, even when we were in Ireland.

'*Téann an fuacht triom,*' my mother would say, shivering, wrapped up in my father's duffel, sitting on the huge boulders that had been brought down to the shore from the quarries by men who were trying to stop the sea from eroding the beach. When he came out of the sea and walked up the beach towards us there was a blue hue to his bald scalp.

Sometimes when I see him now, standing at the foot of my bed, I see him like that: nude and bald and blue.

We moved to Bournemouth when I was five. He got a job teaching German at the Weymouth College of Education, which, the year he joined, became part of Bournemouth Poly. He hated it. He didn't want to teach German. He wanted to teach English. He just wanted to live in England so badly.

Sometimes I can feel his voice. Like a physical feeling inside my brain. But I can't hear it. An irreducible thing. Like an itch that exists an inch below the skin. Like the very last thing that you can hear in a hearing test.

The priest is telling the congregation what is going to happen next. He points to the paschal candle. He points to the tabernacle.

He gestures with an open palm to the little red Formica table beneath the apse where the wedding registry book lies open: a green braided tassel, a fore-edge painting of the wedding at Cana.

I can see that Caroline has crib notes written on her palm in blue ink. I did try to convince her that she wouldn't need to do that. It isn't a test, I told her. I reassured her that the priest would tell us what to do. He would coach us through the ceremony. There was no need to try to memorise any of it.

We'd gone for the marriage preparation programme a few weeks before. We missed the deadline and so we had to do an emergency one. I was expecting it to be like a job interview: a cold room and a stern-looking priest. I was worried about how Caroline would respond. I was relieved when I saw that it was a nice, soft, middle-aged Polish lady who was teaching the course.

On the way out of the building, after the three-hour course, the Polish lady asked us what we would be having for the readings at the ceremony, and I realised then that we hadn't discussed it. I was worried that the woman would take this as an indication that we were not taking the sacrament seriously enough, that her question was a final, secret stumbling block. Instead she just smiled and put her hand on my elbow and told us that a traditional choice would be the story of the wedding at Cana.

I didn't say this to the Polish woman, but actually I wanted to include a reading from Bartholomew Playfere's prophecies, from notebook nine, sometimes referred to as 'The Nightingale Notebook' because of the marginalia: the little scribbled drawings of a nightingale that you can find on verso 20 and recto 25. Later on – when the notebooks were rediscovered and rebound and donated to the British Library – the designers included a gold inlaid design, a drawing of a nightingale, on the front cover.

'Please tell me that you're joking,' Caroline said, when I suggested it. She pulled a sassy expression. She always goes to sassy as a precursor to real irritation.

To my face she said that it was nerdy, but to her friends she boasted about my obsession with Bartholomew Playfere.

'He reads this stuff for *pleasure* mind you,' she would say. 'For pleasure! *Imagínate* amigo.'

She liked the idea that I was a savant. A member of an invisible empire of the unschooled learned. It intrigued her that I had done nothing by the book, because her parents had done everything by the book. They were doctors.

'Do you think that you *love* knowledge?' she asked me once. 'I don't think that I ever knew anyone who really *loves* knowledge the way that you seem to.'

Sometimes, before we were married, she would come over to my mother's house and I would find her in my bedroom leafing through the densely scribbled exercise books that were piled on my desk.

Anyway, we chose the wedding feast at Cana instead.

Only now, sitting next to Caroline in the front pew, listening to Father Edward read the story of the wedding feast at Cana, do I remember sitting next to my father on my bed in the house in Bournemouth – the bedspread with the faded, primary-coloured shapes of dinosaurs on it – while he read from the story of the wedding feast at Cana, and how when he got to the word 'steward' and I asked him what a steward was he couldn't tell me. Days later he told me that it was an attempted translation of an untranslatable ancient Greek word. A word that must have meant something to the evangelist but that does not mean much of anything to anyone any more. A word that might mean something like 'chief partygoer'. *Architriklinos*.

'You know who the *Architriklinos* is in this family?'

'Who?'
'You.'

He meant that I made him laugh. He lulled me into a false sense of security when he roared with laughter at the things that I said or did. Other times he would get angry. Once upon a time my father's sister sent us a jar of raw honey that she had gathered from the beehives that sat behind her farmhouse in Lobbach on the outskirts of Heidelberg. There was a label on the jar, written in Gothic script, which said *Akazienhonig aus der Pfalz*. The honey was pungent. One day somebody left the lid off the jar of honey and by the time we got home from school the pungent aroma had filled the house. I walked into the kitchen and I told my father that the honey smelled like farts. He dragged me out into the garden and made me sit on the back step. I was crying. He told me that my conduct was vulgar. My conduct was intolerably vulgar, he said. I didn't even know what he meant. And – even afterwards, even years later – I *never* understood why he had to take me outside to tell me this. It was as though the jar of honey was an honoured guest, as though he couldn't make a scene in its presence.

I suspect he was just a little worked up, my mother said to me at the time, I suspect he was just feeling a little homesick.

Sometimes I didn't understand what he meant. I didn't understand, either, why the Gospel stories seemed to go straight from Jesus being born to Him being thirty. I didn't understand why Christmas was only a few months before Easter. I didn't understand why the statues of Mary seemed to be the same age when she was in the stable with the infant Jesus as when she was kneeling at the cross or holding His adult body in her arms. And then when my father read to me from *Treasure Island*, events that seemed to be weeks apart would all take place in the course of one evening. Events that all took place on the same day seemed to take place over multiple evenings.

My father refused to believe that I didn't understand that time is different in books. He accused me of being anally retentive. He turned the lights out early. He closed the bedroom door even though I asked him not to. I lay in the dark listening to the wind battering at the windows.

It was windy in Bournemouth.

'*Téann an fuacht tríom,*' my mother said, on the long walk home from the school. I hated that school. The children were all cruel there.

'They aren't cruel,' Caoimhe said to my mother who cradled my head in her arms. 'They don't like him because he tells them that they're all stupid and that he's cleverer than them. That's going to be the same wherever he goes to school.'

Caoimhe wanted to do a reading at the wedding and we were pleased about that until she told us, a few weeks before the wedding, that she had chosen to read a bit from one of my father's poems. In the end we agreed to a compromise. She would read his favourite passage from St Matthew's Gospel.

'And why take ye thought for raiment? Consider the lilies of the field, how they grow; how they toil not, and neither do they spin: and yet Solomon in all his glory was not arrayed like one of these.'

She looks funny, standing up there, reading from the lectern – so solemn – wearing those denim trousers and that tartan shirt. The priest looks abashed. I can hear the rustle of Caroline's American cousin's bashful American husband's polyester trousers as he crosses and uncrosses his legs. I don't want to turn round. I don't want to catch my mother's gaze. I reach my hand down and I squeeze Caroline's hand and she looks at me. I meet her gaze and then turn and catch the gaze of the Eugène de Mazenod statue, staring down at us from the altar. I try to visualise my mother's face, her fixed smile.

'Why would it upset her?' Caoimhe had said, when she first proposed reading my father's poem.

Why would it *upset* her?' I had said.

'What did he do wrong anyway?' she had said. 'What did he do to her that was so terrible in the final analysis? You tell me.'

He quizzed her. She would cry when he did.

He was generous but he hated to be asked for anything. That was the main issue. That was also why he always told my mother that she was demanding. It seemed to him, after all, that she was. He had always given her everything and she had always asked for more.

And even when he left he gave her all of his money: the house, the money, his books, everything. He walked out with just the clothes on his back. That was so she could never complain. It was what he had been doing all along. It was his masterpiece.

The day that he left we got straight on the train from Bournemouth to Holyhead. I was eight. The train was orange. The air was scalding. The seats were orange and red and brown and I was wearing my orange corduroy dungarees. My mother bought us cups of scalding orange-coloured tea from the buffet car. Somehow it was all comforting to me. I felt as though we had all been blown into the air by an explosion, and that we might just keep floating up and up into the universe, untethered by gravity. It was the gravity that I hated. The family felt like gravity to me at that age. It was 1985.

My grandfather's house in Connemara was white, in a green field. The house smelt like mud and milk and bacon. I ran around outside in the field with the half-mad dog and the girl cousins.

'If you fail to matriculate your son before March then he will sacrifice his place for the new term,' said the headmaster's secretary over the phone from Bournemouth. My granny didn't understand. She called my mother over to the phone but my mother was already in a state of convalescence.

My grandfather lifted me up and threw me, weightless, into the air above Connemara. He laughed when he asked how old I was and I told him that I was eight. He didn't believe me.

'*Is bréagadóir é!*' he shouted, everyone laughing, hooting, throwing me into the air. '*Is bréagadóir é!*' ■

DAVID BRANDON GEETING
Clean Apple from *Amusement Park*

THE RECIPE

Rebecca May Johnson

I have never met the person who wrote the recipe, but it is recommended to me on a newspaper website by a cook who has been recommended to me by another cook, whose judgement I trust because I have tasted her food. The route to the recipe is made by tongues.

It is by far the cheapest and easiest recipe in a feature about famous chefs' favourite recipes, but it is precise in ways I do not expect.

During my first performance of the recipe, I have a revelation about ingredients, or vegetables: they are *things*. I must learn to watch them closely, ready to accommodate their whims, which are not human.

The recipe is a method for responding to things. Things have agency in many directions. Like words, they have histories and contexts, but when I perform the recipe, things become other things in a messier transformation than words in a sentence. They spatter my shirt red. The recipe is a text that can produce spattering because it was spattering before it was language. Language is only a holding pattern for the recipe – not its origin, nor its terminus.

Spattering is not mentioned in the recipe. The text does not anticipate the liveliness of the process it describes, which spatters wildly. The substance in the pan trespasses beyond its linguistic boundary, making marks, or mark-making on my shirt, the wall, the dry surface of whatever book is close by. There is always *more*. There is more than has been recorded in the text and there will be more again. Things will be hotter and redder. There will be spattering.

In some ways the recipe text gives me no clue about what is to come. This is hard to forgive. But after cooking it a thousand times, the recipe turns out to be Good Enough. It holds me and it survives my many attempts to destroy it. (D. W. Winnicott)

The second, third, fourth time I make the recipe I follow the instructions as precisely as I can, reverent and still wonderstruck by the transformation of matter in which I am a participant.

My body is changed by the recipe –

after tasting it, I see flavour differently, which means I see *things* differently, because flavour is a quality of things, or can be. And it's not seeing, it's tasting, but it's a tasting that inaugurates a different relationship to things, a new method of perceiving. It is not only the surface I am looking at; I am learning to see *into* things, seeking the dimension of Being that is flavour. There are so many possibilities. Each time I encounter the same thing, the same ingredient, I find that it's different again, again, different again, so the recipe is always a method for seeking.

turn the heat down to very low

On the eighth time of making the recipe I do not add fresh herbs at the end because I have run out of money. The herbs cost more than the rest of the ingredients put together in the small urban supermarket near where I live. It is less fragrant but still intense; it tastes redder.

For my twelfth performance, several months later, I am exhausted from working until 3 a.m. in a pub and I have missed the closing time of the last pizza place that delivers in south London. I decide to free-pour the oil instead of measuring it spoon by spoon. Even while tired I feel the frisson of resistance to the text's specificity and have a small conversation in my head with the author of the recipe where I explain that even though I have not measured the oil, it's probably almost the same.

For the twenty-first performance I change the preparation of the garlic and I don't slice it *very thinly* as the recipe instructs. Instead, imitating the movements of a man I have recently met, I crush it and keep crushing it and crushing with a knife until it is almost a paste, which turns out to be quite difficult and annoying to do, and the taste is different. My tired wrists know the extent of my deviation from the method. The change in method means I can no longer see when the garlic *becomes coloured a pale gold* as the recipe text directs, so I turn to my nose for navigational purposes. This different way of preparing garlic is brought on by a kind of blindness called desire, which drives me off my intended course.

Cutting and slicing is not a matter of dividing one thing into smaller fractions of the same thing; after cutting, it is not the same thing. In Harold McGee's encyclopedia of kitchen science, I read that in the case of garlic and other alliums, when cells are cut, an enzyme trigger is released that interacts with chemical ammunition to produce a pungent sulphurous molecule designed to deter animals from eating them. The taste which attracts us should read as poison. The enzyme reaction in garlic produces a hundredfold higher concentration of molecules than other alliums. Slicing, pounding and crushing do not only change the physical shape of a garlic clove into smaller pieces. Each method alters the very chemistry, the very Being of the clove in a different way. The clove cannot be reassembled or returned to the clove it once was. Form and structure is a matter of Being, too.

During the thirtieth performance I enthusiastically tell a new housemate (the first I have had) what the recipe has taught me about the thermodynamics of oil. On a low heat oil rises slowly until it *floats free*, gleaming and tinted red. The oil cooks the garlic gently and circulates its sweetness. Stirring too vigorously can emulsify the oil with other liquids in the pan and prevent it from moving in this special way.

In the fortieth performance I am cooking for someone who likes capers and chilli and so I add capers and chilli flakes. Even though I know that capers are not integral to the recipe and that they are not written in the recipe and that this addition in some ways violates the principles of the recipe, when we eat, we can taste capers and heat and that is what they wanted. Capers are a challenge for my childish palate because it is not long since I left home, and my mother does not like capers and does not put them in her cooking.

The year I begin cooking the recipe is the year I go to a famous hairdressing school and let an experimental stylist cut off all my hair. They do not charge a fee, and I am in need of a new direction, an escape route from my body, which has begun to feel altogether too constricting. *Directional* is what they call their haircuts – just what I need! The experimental hairdresser is an intense east Londoner in her forties and deeply focused on her art. My hair becomes the medium with which she works to produce a new cut, a new dish. She tends to my hair in the way that the recipe encourages me to tend to ingredients, responding to their qualities, their potential for transformation. She likes that the hairs on my head are fine but abundant so she can create volume and achieve great height without the weight of the hair causing collapse. She describes this to audiences who are watching her and writing down the recipe, planning to bring these techniques to their home salons, like a cookery demonstration.

All that is required of me when she cuts my hair is to sit still for hours and hours, sometimes up to eight hours. My phone gets no signal in the basement salon, and I let my mind wander. The hairdresser does not require me to speak, or to say 'I'; she just needs me to sit, silent and unmoving. It is very freeing to be this way. I become a body without words, present only as a medium, willingly manipulated. I let her cut my hair again and again, sometimes on a stage while someone talks and points at my head, sometimes in a teaching salon. But even when on stage, I am not required to be a subject. It takes hours of concentration for her to produce brave new shapes with my hair using scissors, combs, heat and air. She collaborates with colourists who participate in constructing the haircuts. They spend hours painting my hair and folding it up in foil and when they unwrap it, vibrant abstract images have appeared on my head. Each colour changes how the light will filter through the manifold textures she has produced. She makes smooth curves or pointillist stubble or rough clashing waves that reach great crescendos; long single strands and thick blocks refract light at different frequencies. I am struck when the hairdresser refers to my hair as 'virgin' onstage during a demonstration. She means undyed, but the erotic dimension of our strange relationship does not escape me. She appears in several dreams.

After the first cut with the experimental hairdresser, I find I can breathe more easily, and more easily still each time after that. I did not grow up at a time when popular culture accepted that people should have autonomy over their appearance. *What Not to Wear* is the mantra we were encouraged to repeat to ourselves, learnt from the wildly popular BBC television series that launched in 2001, when I was fifteen. Body parts including legs and arms and stomachs, body hair, displays of 'masculine muscles', unfeminine haircuts, and above all fat are prodded and condemned by presenters on the violently normative and fat-phobic TV show. When I let the stylist experiment with my hair, I begin to feel released from something constraining and oppressive. Like the recipe, the haircuts change the relationship between words and things for me. The experimental hairdresser gives me the knowledge that I can remake my body, again and again. It becomes a space for play, exploration and deviation.

Each time I cook the recipe differently, my hair is different too –

> There is the time I make the recipe after my long brown hair has been cut into an asymmetric shape with a shaved side, a bob on the other side, and a thin 'veil' of hair at the back.

> Two weeks later they have dyed my hair dark auburn and black and purple at the front.

> Several months after that I cook with deep pink hair with a pale pink fringe and black marks drawn onto my face.

> Then it becomes bright red and a spherical bob with a slight asymmetry, after Vidal Sassoon.

The people I have recently moved in with love comic books and cosplay and make-up and Zelda and making their own porn and horror films and foxes and Halloween parties and watching all of *Buffy the Vampire Slayer* from start to finish and I love them and take out a standing order at a comic-book shop too. They like the hairstyles I come home with, whatever they are, and love whatever clothes I wear and whatever make-up I try and will come and queue with me for whatever obnoxious club night with a 'no look no entry' policy that I am obsessed with. They let me cook excitable meals for them even though sometimes I fill the house with smoke or spray it with mushroom soup when the blender explodes; I teach them the recipe.

The trick is to slow-cook

For the seventieth performance my anxiety causes me to turn the heat up too high. I hurry things. I have retreated into myself and fail to keep faith with the ingredients. I interfere and force my will on the ingredients and forget that it is a collaboration. The excess heat I apply has the effect of a weapon; it is wounding. The flavour at the end lacks sweetness and depth and I have to repair the dish, inventing ways to accommodate my impatience. The damage I visit upon the ingredients must be repaired with new ingredients: *I add sugar and a half teaspoon of vinegar.*

When I think about performing the recipe I think about the movements of subatomic particles or the orbits of moons and planets, there is a physics to it. The recipe introduces me to principles of touch, knife work, heat and time. The temporality of white becoming gold in oil. I must be careful about how I move my hands, the interventions they make can be significant, they are always in relation. In the study of electrons nothing is ignored because everything can have an effect, even looking. The proverb 'a watched pot never boils' was taken up by physicists trying to find ways to describe the behaviour of quantum particles. 'Watched pot behaviour' is another term for the Zeno effect in quantum physics, whereby frequent measurement inhibits the process being observed from actually taking place. Sometimes my anxiety or impatience causes me to take the pan off the heat too soon.

Cooking often hovers at the fringes of serious thought. I see it used as metaphor in philosophical texts, invoked in introductory paragraphs, deployed to convey the complexity of processes that are not cooking. But I find I need to draw on all available resources to articulate the complexity of the recipe. After ten years or more of experimentation

I have not exhausted its possibilities; I have not found a limit for what the recipe can teach me about being in the world.

The recipe is a method of navigation, a method for seeing or seeking what is beyond me.

The recipe makes a space in my life where time does not pass but accumulates as a hot red sea full of feeling, good and bad.

The month before I move to Berlin to study and work, I perform the recipe and my hair is even shorter and red with a blue-and-blonde fringe; blue quickly fades to grey.

For the first performance of the recipe in Berlin my hair is white blonde and I have painted the top half of my face pink, I am drunk, and I play Giorgio Moroder, whose music I have recently started listening to. I put my favourite apron over my clothes; it is checked green and orange and is made from pliable cotton and I pull it tight. In this apron I orchestrate many large meals. I become a conductor of chopping and frying and drinking and dancing.

For the third performance of the recipe in Berlin my hair is still white blonde. I am wearing blue lipstick with dark blue glitter over the top, affixed with lip gloss, and dramatic black eyebrows painted much higher than my own on my forehead, black eyeliner, a drawn-on beauty spot, and a blue leotard. The more artificial I look the better it feels, being not essentially anything. At 3 a.m. I go to the club Berghain with my friends and we queue in the snow and then dance to pounding techno until 11 a.m., which counts as an early bedtime for many attendees.

When I am not in nightclubs or cooking in the apartment, I wander the city alone wearing large headphones. The headphones make a space for me that is insulated from social interactions. Most nights when I am not out I wake up at 4 or 5 a.m. in a panicked alcohol sweat and call the very patient person I am seeing long-distance in the UK. Apart from my Norwegian flatmate with whom I spend most of my time, a philosophy graduate I recognise in a nightclub from a London library, the owner of the fashion store I work in and a customer whom I befriend, the only people I speak to are those with few enough boundaries to make it past my headphones.

The philosophy graduate from Scotland picks the meat from a chicken I have cooked and talks about an ex-girlfriend and Throbbing Gristle and who he wants to fuck now – he's sure they'll be out this week. When we have drunk everything in the flat we leave to be in the perfect and blessed light of Berlin nightclubs where I dance until the make-up runs down my face. A tall and beautiful man called Vladimir is on the door of the club that becomes like home for a short, sweet while. Peaches sings 'Fuck the Pain Away' from a podium with her pubic hair spewing gloriously from her sequinned leotard, free blue packs of Gauloises cigarettes are handed out to everyone. A French man with a moustache called Charlie Le Mindu is shaving heads for fifteen euros in the basement. We exit at 4 a.m. to eat a kebab, and then go back in to dance again, or perhaps onwards to Berghain. Every dance floor is an ecstatic exploration of our desires, our bodies.

The two hundredth time I make the recipe is a kind of madness. Cooking becomes a social support I lean on too heavily. A German teenager in my literature class at the university manages to strike up a conversation, declaring her admiration for my tight red jeans. Unprepared and taken aback, I give a freakish and exaggerated performance of social courtesy and promise to cook a meal for all her friends for her birthday at my apartment without asking my flatmates. She is local and lives with her parents and treats the occasion as a chance to go wild. I feel hysterical as I serve food to dozens of people I have never met who flood the apartment, play music I don't like and intrude on my flatmates' private space. I find out that I do not like the girl whose birthday party I am hosting, that I do not know her at all; we do not really speak again after that night. Even worse, I make a fatal substitution in the recipe, not anticipating how differently the ingredient would behave. The thought of all these strangers eating the manic, bad dish haunts me painfully.

When the temperature is so low that the cold burns my face I buy a bag of oranges from Lidl. I take one out. It is an orange against drinking and against the lost feeling I can't shake. I buy the webbed bag of fruit as a tonic, as a way of following advice that I have not received for years. It is a way of following my mother's advice even if it has never been given, a dream of good advice, which I plan to absorb with each segment. I peel the orange hopefully, like it will be a doctor, an oracle, a cure, but when I gaze full of hope into the wet orange flesh it moves. The orange flesh moves, wriggles and is alive and I am not hallucinating. The orange is full of maggot larvae. The oranges are the birthplace of decay whose life was throbbing evidence against mine and I scream and throw it against the wall in the kitchen and it splats and sprays orange juice and larvae all over, running into each other in drips down the wall. I have never been more shocked. I eat no more oranges that winter.

In London again I make the recipe and my hair is a short bowl cut, dyed deep burgundy red.

Then I dye it black and shave an undercut, too. When I cook, as when I walk around the city, I wear a long, black blazer over buttoned-up shirts with black platform boots. My lipstick is bright orange or blue or black or purple, any colour but red.

However, while I love clothes and make-up, I am beginning to use them like a carapace, a hard shell to protect myself from other people, from the vulnerability of intimacy. I set too much store by appearances and control mine too tightly.

Cooking is the tool I use to draw close to other people, though closeness makes me anxious. Cooking is how I manage closeness. Sometimes it can go wrong, like the stranger's birthday party in Berlin. Cooking for someone is not always an appropriate response to meeting them.

But sometimes, it's OK.

For the two hundred and fortieth performance, four years after I first made the recipe, I make it for you:

> at least there is that *You*, which is every beloved, which constitutes itself across difference and species and the whole of life. *You* is eros and caritas all mixed up in a word. It is also the stranger who any of us might be, and in that the only law is probably love, and that the violation of life anywhere is the violation of life everywhere, and in that no one is free until everyone is, *You* is what everything in the world is staked on, including yourself. (Anne Boyer)

You teach me about cooking for every other Other; you teach me about 'that *You*'.

You are almost a stranger – we haven't known each other long – but I stake myself on cooking for you.

You tell me that some ingredients disagree with you, there are certain things you cannot eat, but you can eat everything in the recipe. So I make it for you once, and you love it, and then I make it for you a hundred times.

Years later you say you would like to eat the recipe as your last meal, and that sometimes when we are apart, you type my first name and the title of the recipe into an internet search, which of course doesn't turn up anything useful.

When I am thinking about what to cook for you, I return to the recipe as a meditative practice, to the beginning of what I know you can eat. Your appetite changes the recipe over time; I ask what else you want, and I change the recipe to make something that is new and also the same.

For the three hundred and sixty-fifth performance of the recipe I add things that make it sweet and sour and spiced and serve it with lamb patties to evoke a meal we ate with our friends by a river several summers before. Now we are in the city and it is not warm, but when we eat that evening, we are drunk by the river again.

> *Here again here again here again,*
> *the recipe becomes an ensemble performance.*

Writing recipes for you is the beginning of my writing. I begin writing so you will have recipes when you need them – when I am not there. In periods when I stop writing recipes, which is also when I have felt most distant from myself, most anxious, you ask me to write again and say that you miss it. So, I begin again. I am able to do very little without being asked, unable to see a reason why. What purpose would it serve? Your appetite, your asking summons a subject again and again, often just as it is – as I am – fading.

When we do not see each other often and live in different places, I cook a dish for you even though you are not there and have not asked, so that I can write down the new recipe and send it to you.

The original wording of the recipe, which I have not read in many years, recedes in my mind although all of my movements and decisions are shaped by it and are in relation to it, even as they are different.

For the four hundred and fifty-first performance I make the recipe then I use it as the basis for a different dish for two women. Both are hot.

There is sexual tension in circulation that I cannot yet articulate. I am in a bad relationship with a man who lives far away, and I am unhappy. I sublimate my feelings into cooking. We eat and then squash together on a sofa to watch a trippy American TV series, the room shimmering with desire. I write a recipe for the dish during the first month of writing down recipes on a website I have made.

The five hundred and third performance of the recipe is wretched. I barely want to eat the dish. I am so paralysed by the fear of failure that writing even one word of my PhD makes it difficult to breathe. I struggle for several hours to get off the sofa before I can cook. I am only able to get off the sofa and cook because a friend rings me and tells me to do so. A ball of sadness and anxiety burns in my torso, making it difficult to taste my food.

I have the feeling that the balance between words and things is off, that words have been mapped onto the world, constraining its wild potential into a narrow use of language. The asymmetry of the word-world relationship bothers me like a physical irritation. For example, the word 'woman', about which I can't say more than *it doesn't sit right with me*. It feels like a closed semantic circuit limiting the way I walk, move my hands and my face, use my voice. I want to crack it open, refuse it. I have the urgent desire to sever the bond between the word and my body, my life. What else might I become?

While studying literature and philosophy we look closely at language and its effects, what it does. I find that words have been used like maps to impose order from above. Sometimes writers use language to make it seem like certain forms of knowledge are not knowledge at all, or to make it seem like certain forms of life are not really life. The forms of knowledge and of life that are diminished in the texts we study are almost always attributed to women. In my experience of higher education, conversations about what counts as 'serious thought' situate the recipe outside of the space of intellectual enquiry.

When it comes to cooking, the academy is at sea.

But I have also been blind to my own knowledge-making practices, to my own research. I have not seen the knowledge that the recipe gives me as part of 'what I know'.

The six hundred and fiftieth time I make the recipe I make a space in the sauce halfway through cooking and break in two eggs because it is the morning, and in the morning by this point in my mid-twenties, I eat eggs for breakfast. I eat eggs for breakfast because several years ago I lived in Berlin with people who ate eggs for breakfast. Imitating the egg-eating of the people I lived with in Berlin enables me slowly to overcome a childhood fear and dislike of eggs.

I discover that many people have a strong feeling of connection with eggs; eggs are a good, even inexhaustible, topic for conversation.

Someone I meet from a dating website tells me about the American food writer M.F.K. Fisher. I read her book *How to Cook a Wolf* and admire the thought: 'Probably one of the most private things in the world is an egg until it is broken.' (M.F.K. Fisher)

Fisher continues:

> Until then, you would think its secrets are its own, hidden behind the impassive beautiful curvings of its shell, white or brown or speckled. It emerges full-formed, almost painlessly [The *egg* may not be bothered, but nine years and two daughters after writing this I wonder somewhat more about the hen. I wrote, perhaps, too glibly.] from the *hen*. It lies without thought in the straw, and unless there is a thunderstorm or a sharp rise in temperature it stays fresh enough to please the human palate for several days.

I like Fisher's concern for the hen who lays the eggs. Fisher thinks of the egg-worker.

There is a long period when, channelling my new-found delight in egg-eating, I crack eggs into the pan. The egg version of the recipe develops its own life. I find that I can give ten people breakfast at once by baking large serving dishes, or make a lunch for one friend to eat with bread.

At one point I begin, then abandon, an essay about the TV detective Columbo and eggs, in which I theorise that Columbo is an egg.

> In the episode 'Murder by the Book', directed by Steven Spielberg, Columbo wears his eggshell-coloured raincoat and makes an omelette in a suspect's kitchen. He moves manically round the room, muttering a recipe to himself – 'cheese, and onions and, um, butter, cheese and, err, I need something to, ah, grate the cheese' – and cracks eggs until the suspect becomes an egg and cracks too and brings the conversation back to the crime, revealing herself. In other episodes, Columbo produces a hard-boiled (ha ha) egg from his raincoat pocket to eat for breakfast, which he says he prefers with salt. Sometimes he carries a salt shaker in the pockets of his coat. The ordinary but uncanny intimacy brokered by the eggs affects the suspects much like the presence of Columbo. There is an inevitability to the cracking of an egg. If you see it, you know it will be cracked; they see him break the egg on the tyre iron, they know they will be cracked too. Columbo remains unknown and uncracked in his eggshell raincoat. He is the egg who will crack you. He uses eggs to gesture to his inner life, telling stories about a wife we never meet while remaining 'the most private thing in the world'. The suspects are eggs, Columbo is an egg, the eggs are eggs . . .

. . . I am rapidly losing control of the narrative.

Eggs provoke speculation that spirals out of control.

I make the egg version of the recipe all over the place and for so many people and I change the egg recipe, too. I add:

potatoes
onion
peppers
sausage
spiced sausage
lardons
coriander
spinach
and garnish with
garlic yogurt
spiced butter
Turkish chilli flakes
fresh herbs
and more I cannot remember.

Finally, the egg dish becomes as overwrought as a late-Victorian house with too many turrets.

The eight hundred and ninetieth time, I make the recipe because I have nothing else in the cupboard and I have run out of money. I am bored of it, and I don't want to eat it; I resent it.

The recipe has spattered my clothes and the wall and cookbooks and my computer; it has also spattered other books. Sometimes I am cooking because I am turning away from my PhD about a rewriting of the *Odyssey* by German poet Barbara Köhler. Often, I am not waving but drowning. As part of my study, I read

Dialectic of Enlightenment (1944) by German philosophers Theodor Adorno and Max Horkheimer. In it, they present Odysseus' epic journey and the challenges he overcomes as an allegory for the development of the 'rational' subject. In Odysseus' attempts to defeat various feminine, monstrous and natural Others on his journey, Adorno and Horkheimer see a subject who wants to master the 'uncivilised' aspects of life. Odysseus reaches the ironic conclusion that the greatest threat to life is the vital quality of embodied life itself, which is too emotional and too unreliable to be predicted and controlled.

Life is too much like spattering! Not enough like language!

In the eight hundredth performance of the recipe, I use butter instead of oil. It smells sweet and musky instead of grassy and peppery and I do it because I want to feel rich and erotic and it works. I have a new friend who makes it in this way, and I imitate her gestures. Through imitating her gestures, I find out something new about flavour that reading the recipe text alone does not reveal.

Odysseus is a logocentrist; he favours 'language or words to the exclusion or detriment of the matters to which they refer'. *(Oxford English Dictionary)* When he encounters the Sirens, creatures who are half-bird, half-woman, Odysseus wants to hear their song because it contains knowledge of everything that has happened on the Earth. He wants to have the Sirens' knowledge for himself, but he wants it without hazarding his body. As he approaches the Sirens, Odysseus ties himself to the mast of his ship and blocks his rowers' ears with wax, hoping to listen and survive. He will not put his skin in the game. He listens to their song from afar and the rowers keep the ship moving past.

In the nine hundred and twenty-first performance, a decade after the first, I leave out the garlic and add anchovies and rosemary or *rosmarinus* or 'dew of the sea', and then at the end I add double cream because I want to be overtaken by silken intensity and fragrance, a kind of transcendence, and that is what I feel. In a moment of ecstasy as its flavour courses through my body, I call the recipe a goddess.

The knowledge of all things is embedded in the effects of the Sirens' song on the listener's body. Sailors are physically drawn to the Sirens when they sing, and therein lies the danger. But when Odysseus ties his body to the mast of the boat and sails by without moving closer, he breaks the connection between their song and the body of the listener. The Sirens' words lose their bond to the physical world when Odysseus seizes their knowledge and disregards the presence it commands. To avoid the danger of his own desire Odysseus holds the world at arm's length and language 'begins to pass over into designation . . .' (Adorno and Horkheimer, trans. Jephcott) Knowing becomes looking and pointing from a distance.

I realise that in the kitchen I am grappling with the same questions as in my academic study. When I cook the recipe, I experience the difference between the knowledge promised by language, and the unboundedness of embodiment, which is both richer and more dangerous that the text can convey. And sometimes, like Odysseus, I distance myself from other people, from desire, from intimacy. How much should I hazard? Sometimes I want more control than is possible, so I hide rather than risk the vulnerability of proximity.

Can I know a recipe without cooking it?

The more I think about it, the more I think Odysseus is tricking himself. The Sirens' song is information that is known through an ecstatic collision of words and bodies. It is an invitation to a way of knowing that includes the emergent liveliness of things. Even though he extracts the Sirens' language, Odysseus cannot receive the knowledge contained in their song because he does not partake of it with his body. By refusing to accept the song as a physical event, Odysseus can only access an abstract version of what it imparts. It is as if Odysseus reads the recipe text but never cooks it. For the Sirens, knowledge is not separable from the song, from singing. I cannot know the recipe text until I cook it.

Cooking by the recipe a thousand times and more gives me this insight into language and its relation to living things.

A recipe that is 'distanced from any particular content which fulfils it' (Adorno and Horkheimer, trans. Jephcott) is a joke, is irrational, because it feeds no body.

A recipe that feeds nobody has no future.

Before the recipe was a text it was written by the body: it was cooked. The recipe bears the traces of its corporeal origins by remaining in the service of the body. Without a body (and bodies, things, ingredients) a recipe text makes no sense.

The ethics of the recipe text arise from its proximity to life, to hungry bodies.

The recipe is always gathering life into itself, gathering words and things and people together, again and again. Rolled-up sleeves. How will life continue? Like this, like this, here and there and then and now.

Thinking about the many realities that have unfolded through the scant language of the recipe, I can see words as capacious again, as shifting over time through being cooked again, again, again, differently.

The recipe shows me time as material change. The recipe establishes a correspondence between material change and language, between time and language.

The recipe means that time is no longer divisible like empty abstract space. (Bergson via Deleuze)

The recipe intends life: language surviving through the body, which eats with a different appetite each day.

There is the body and bodies who have produced the recipe and the bodies that it serves, a recipe is a text that is *for*, for the pleasure of *You*, you, them.

The recipe only returns at the request of the body.

The recipe serves at the pleasure of the body.

The recipe text will always be specific, or be made specific, and is in dialogue with specific appetites. The recipe is rewritten by the people to whom it attends.

Descriptions of people cooking always move me so much, I think this is why.

In the philosophy and theory I study, the movement of life into language appears again and again as a kind of hollowing out, a loss. A loss of the kind that Odysseus both suffers and inflicts. I do not find a way beyond this impasse until I begin to think through the recipe, until I devote myself to thinking with it. The recipe offers something else; not a nothing at the end of writing, but life returned to language a thousand times over.

The recipe is my epic (and yours too). The recipe is the ship and the hot red sea. In the recipe epic life is measured in spoons of sauce. Again and again the recipe brings me 'that *You*' (Boyer) who is also every you in particular. You are the beginning of my writing, of my epic.

*

The thousandth performance of the recipe takes place after speaking to you on the phone.

You tell me you feel anxious and panicky. We have been living through a global pandemic for six months and I have not seen you in person for almost a year. By chance you will be close by at the weekend to see your mother, who is not well. I measure out the oil spoon by spoon as I have not done for several years and follow the written instructions as precisely as I am able. My hands are shaky, and I hold onto the recipe text to navigate. I make double quantities, because I feel like that is what is needed, and pour it into a glass jar that I have sterilised. I carry the tomato sauce with me as I travel to meet you. When I hand it to you your partner says, Oh, is that some kind of special sauce? I say, I just know that you like it. Later on, you tell me that I have given you love in the form of tomato sauce.

I cook the sauce hundreds of times with the thought that I might be making you; then I realise that you have made me. ■

POPPY PROMISES

Thomas Duffield

Our home was a static caravan, sat quietly in a field with walls entangled with ivy, on a small farm where my mother and father began to raise my sister and me. During this time my father struggled with a heroin addiction. However difficult it may have been for my mother and father, to my memory we had a charmed life growing up. As children, my father's addiction was not discussed, and after he left, years passed with little contact. In 2016 I started meeting with my father regularly, offering support as he underwent a detox. When we were together we talked about nothing in particular.

Six years have now passed by and I still meet up with my father regularly, drinking coffee from the same two cups. After a long and difficult winter he is once again going through another detox programme, collecting methadone from the pharmacy up the street. It is hard to watch him grow older in this way, lighter in his pocket, looking for things to smoke. Living as if he insists upon fading away. When I dare to look at my own life in the same way, things are not so different. Two steps forward and one step back. Both my father and I have pebbles in our shoes.

Beginning to reconcile with his past in a way that is mischievous, yet sincere, my father uses the term 'poppy promises' to describe the empty promises that he reluctantly makes in order to score heroin. With a glimmer of humour in his eye, he relayed to me the story of a disagreement between himself and a dealer: 'I know I said I'd pay, but that was just a poppy promise. I'd swap my grandma for some heroin if I needed it.' He quickly reassured me that he wouldn't trade in my great-grandma, but was using it to illustrate a point. He was proud of his lyricism, and so was I; his words stuck with me all afternoon. I thought about all the poppy promises made to my mother over the years my parents were together, as they began building a life with each other and raising children. It was these poppy promises that ultimately led them down different paths in life, and, while my sister and I were young, made it difficult for us to understand our father.

Now, as my father comes closer to retirement age, I have become an adult myself. Figuring out what it means to be a man in the north of England, I've questioned how many men have lost themselves through an inability to be vulnerable. How many of us would sooner turn to drink, drugs or destruction before admitting that we are scared and don't know what to do about it. I asked my dad, 'When you're old enough to draw a pension, do you think you'll spend your pension on a draw?' He laughed a little, and rolled a spliff. He's never offered me any drugs, but he has bought me a few pints in our time together.

When I first reached out to my father in 2016, I had expected to simply walk into his life and make a series of portraits that documented our relationship. I was unaware of how slow and challenging this project would be. I thought things would be easy, but instead they were hard. I wandered in circles, sometimes orbiting closer and other times retreating further away. Too nervous to open up to him about my ambitions for this project, and to ask to make his portrait, I spent four years listening to the stories he shared instead. Scared he would say no, and still unsure if the work was worthwhile, I thought that maybe it was foolish to try and give this experience a form to inhabit; as if it could live within pictures. How strange it is to leave home for university and to come back with a lens. To make a subject of the very same entity I am a part of, to be outside and within it.

I was frustrated at my inability to open up to my father, and would return to our old family home empty-handed, making still-life photographs instead. Blurring the lines between the staged and the observed, these images attempt to communicate the challenging emotional landscape that is present within families that experience addiction. The tensions that run beneath the surface, the highs, lows and occasional calamities. Moving back to the farm where I grew up, I began working with my mother who still lives there today. She was a single parent for many years, leaning on my grandparents from time to time. She found a job as a reprographics technician at our local school so she could finish at the same time we did. Keeping the house from falling apart and making sure she was around for us, she carried so much weight that my sister and I didn't feel any upon our shoulders.

Unknowingly echoing patterns from the past, she was now once again standing in as a proxy for my father; participating in portraits between her formal employment and domestic chores. An ever-willing participant, present in his absence. At first, I thought of the photographs I made of her as expressions of gratitude, gifts to my mother. Naive, I failed to realise that she is the one gifting her presence to me; giving as though she hasn't been generous enough already. When I look at the photographs now, I am reminded of how much I have yet to learn about love and sacrifice.

I've encountered my own flaws throughout the making of this work, and I've come to believe that we cannot outrun our human frailties. There is so much I want to say to my father, but I struggle to get the words out. Too many times I have tasted the truth on the tip of my tongue and swallowed it down with silence. I've tried to teach myself to walk this Earth like a man, but when I sit by his side I'm a boy again. Despite our shortcomings we still find time to see each other. Through the years I have gotten to know my father better. When I was younger, this was all I wanted, and I am happy that I've had the chance to know him. Over the past six years he has taught me more than I could have ever hoped. ■

Hi Tom if you have your camera wouldnt mind a record of my barley got some nice Ruhbarb spare. X
If you could bring the hair trimmers too if none of possible i understand Tom

Yeah that's all fine now worries and there your hair clippers - I'll bring them back so you can have a trim x

Thanks Tom dont know how you put up with me some dad i hope i can be around long enough to prove i ainte all negative got some pluses x

—

Any luck finding those clippers Dad x

Found them Tomx

Lovely I'll swing around and get my ears lowered X

—

Going for a run dad I'm streamlined

Dont bump into anybody ffs scary man. Lol x

Did you have a good run Whats the verdict on hair doo gand will be impressed proper hair cut

All good everyone saying i look like you

Tiss true handsome fuckers

Theres a song called were is my mind its been looping in my head forgot which group did it but its a good tune and music is a healer

—

Its a tune from a band called the pixies

Hope all ok tom x

I know that song it's at the end of fight club - have you seen that film ?

And all good thanks Dad, how are you ?

I have and i didnt sleep again but been eating feel knackerd but im feeling bit better thanks but been run down my imunity is low so trylng not to catch anything long time without sleep take care all x

Get a stomach full of some scran and see if you can get some sleep weather is going to get nice again at the weekend never let your stomach know youve had a bad day as gand would say

—

I'm sad at moment Tom my lovely potatoes have got blight fucking sad it happens but shame

Sorry about your potatoes, did you lift them up x

I've got to pull the tops so they won't get bigger and they won't keep so I will give some away which is a nice thing to do don't want waste you get my drift hope you aren't feeling to bad Tom x

Had chilly pork sausage from coo op
there 2 50 for 6 but fucking nice Tom.
With roast onion you know caramalised
toms n chips n sweetcorn washed down
with guiness n splif. Content friday tom
say hello to Silvana x

Sounds like a good Friday dad ha
will send your regards cheers dad

—

Thunderstorm x

Hows it going tom am sat by my
fire watching a pair of barn owls
hunting in flood plain area opposite
me there ace to watch

I'm good thank you Dad. How
are you ? Sounds like better
entertainment than the tv.

I think worth a photo of barn owls
was talking to a man today
ive seen him last few days with
a big camera.with zoom lens
looked the part but his stalking
method was shit he thank me for
my feed back and he stood out less
im sure he will get the shots
of the birds they look good z

—

Been ruff my fuck up but getting
to grips with it about time i hope
mentaly and physical i know got it
in me just have to put myself thru
allot of unnessery crap for some
reason guess need too uncover
the demons too fix stuff but im
coming to terms with my let downs
been sad glad you are all ok x

We all love you & I'm certainly
lucky to have you knowing that
you are always Proud of me
and Rach - letting us be ourselves.
Some families look perfect on the
outside but there can be bitterness
between people. I think we all have
a lot of understanding and love
between us

Feels chilly in my house im wearing
my coat could do with some calories
on not good been thin Tom when i get
more finantialy stable boy am going
to eat like the majority must be nice
to open the cubourd and see sumat
a choice to scran be like heaven i
shouldnt be envious of all these
slightly obese people but i am x

Understandable in these times
Dad don't need to apologise,
I'll swing by while I've got the car
tomorrow speak now or hold your
peace lol drop some bread milk
and bacon keep you going till the
money comes x

I will check my bank ballence tomorrow
tom know how things lie thanks for the
offer very kind i will text you late morning
i like to hold my peace god willing x

Sounds good dad I'll leave it
with you x

700 calories the pizza was ace my
belly has not shrunk i could easily
eat another one my appetite is crazy
got spuds baked beans and some
nice chilly sausages for tea with slices
of nice bread mmm nice i shall have
to slow down tom otherwise i will be
spending all my money on food end up
your weigh Get some fat round my organs
have a good son n safe journey in the
morning x

Have a good day sorry that text
got fucked upx

Tom when I snuff it hopefully not
for a bit I want you to take care
of that nice felling axe you kindly
got the handle for it's nice that ace
head it's fucking weighty and it was
my dads grandads so too you it's
  For fucks sake I've had a joint
so I'm going to eat my Pizza

Will do dad family heirloom isn't it
Sounds like a nice evening dad
was it some dawg
X

It is Tom and a good axe and it's
dawg I got to smoke it makes a
good spliff very relaxing lol

Tom if you ever get the chance
listen to Granchester Meadows
of album uma guma by Pink Floyd
lowed with headphones if possible
it's Mint

I'll do that now dad I've got some
good headphones

Nice acoustic guitar and the way the
duck takes of the water clever stereo
for the sixties

Yes that was great I enjoyed that,
and is it a fly or a bee on the stereo
too funny I was just sat in billy wood
today in the long grass was abit
similar

—

Happy Father's Day dad xx

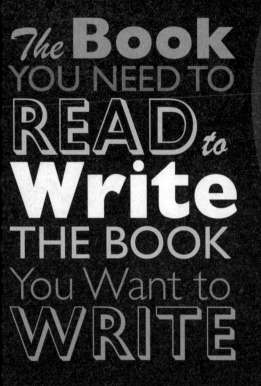

CONSTANTINE CHRISTOFIDES
Janet Malcolm at the University of Michigan in the 1950s

SKROMNOST[1]

Janet Malcolm

T his snapshot is the only memento I have of a girl I was in love
with when I was in my late teens. She is the smiling blond
near the center of the photograph. When I say I was in love with
her, I am speaking from later knowledge. At the time – the late
1940s – girls in love with other girls didn't recognize what was
staring them in the face. They – we – thought you could be in love
only with boys. Lesbianism was something you only heard about.
There was a book called *The Well of Loneliness*, a forbidden, rather

---

[1] *Skromnost* (Czech): modesty, humility, unpretentiousness.

boring text, from which we formed the idea of lesbians as unhappy jodhpur-wearing daughters of fathers who had wanted sons.

Pat Patrick, as the blond was called, was small and compactly built, a Jean Arthur type, who radiated a kind of self-containment and forthrightness that contrasted sharply with the wobbly unsureness of the rest of us. The group picture was of the participants in a six-week-long summer program for American and foreign college students run by an organization called the Lisle Fellowship, whose purpose was to make the world a better place through vapid discussions in the evening and volunteer work during the day. How could it not succeed? But, of course, our main interest was in each other, in forming romantic attachments that took hold for a week or so and then petered out. My (unacknowledged) crush on Pat lasted the entire six weeks. I loved the way she strode about the place, as if she were on her way to a meeting of the Council of Landowners. I loved the way she swore. 'Christ on a crutch!' 'Goodness, gracious, goodness, Agnes!' The word 'uninhibited' was in vogue at the time, and I used it in thinking about Pat, envying as well as admiring her for her freedom from the dull conventions by which I was bound. She was nice to me. I was younger than everyone else – I wasn't in college yet. My mother had learned of the program from one of her friends in the good-doing world, and no one at Lisle seemed to have noticed anything untoward on the application she sent in. I remember Pat counseling me about the boy, Jack, with whom I was going. She didn't like him and I began to see what she meant. I switched to a nicer boy from South America, named Gilberto. Pat was going with someone from France whose name I don't remember, who seemed older and was just possibly worthy of her.

After the summer I saw Pat one more time. In my memory of the meeting she is standing on the sidewalk on Fifth Avenue across the street from the Plaza Hotel. There is to be a reunion in the Village with some of the Lisle people. It is early evening in late summer. Pat is wearing an elegant dress of dark blue taffeta with a gathered skirt and cinched waist and suede pumps. Her hair is arranged in a loose chignon at the back of her neck. I had never seen her looking like this before. During the summer she wore shorts and cotton shirts and a ponytail. She looked like everyone else. Now she looks like a socialite, a daughter of wealth and privilege. She is not at ease. She tells me that she has to go to some event with her aunt, with whom she's staying at the Plaza, and won't be able to go down to the Village.

What interests me now in thinking about this last glimpse of Pat is my lack of surprise at her transformation. Of course she would be wearing that dress and those pumps and have an aunt who was staying at the Plaza. The shock was of recognition. We know so much that we don't know we know about each other. We always know each other's class. On some level I had always known Pat was rich and upper-class. Where I belonged in the money and class divide was equally clear to me.

Our family was ordinary mid-century professional middle-class, neither rich nor poor, with no social pretensions. In Prague my parents had been somewhat better off financially and had ties to an advanced intellectual community. A few of their fellow refugees went back to Czechoslovakia at the end of the war to try to resume their old lives. My parents knew almost from the start that they would stay here. This country is so nonchalantly seductive! There is no escaping its wiles. My father was scarcely off the boat when he became a Dodgers fan.

We lived according to our means, on my parents' salaries, with an easy modesty. The Czech word *skromnost* means 'modesty', but it also carries a mild sense of forelock-tugging humbleness, of knowing one's place. My father worked as a physician and then as a psychiatrist at the Veterans Administration, and my mother worked as an announcer at the Voice of America. We never borrowed money. The idea of 'having money', like rich people did, was alien to us. There was a girl in my class in junior high school named Astrid who lived on Park Avenue and was considered weird because of it. Everyone else lived east of Third Avenue, in what was then working-class Yorkville.

By the same token, I knew that we were a class above the people
who lived in the tenements – we lived in a six-story apartment
building built just before the war – though this knowledge came to
me only gradually. In the earliest years of my childhood in Yorkville,
I had a different idea of the divide between us and the other families
in the neighborhood: I thought we were inferior. I envied the girls
their brightly colored Sunday clothes and their white communion
dresses. I was ashamed of my mother when she came to school
assemblies in the clothes she had worn as a professional woman in
Prague, which I thought dowdy and poor compared with the shiny
flower-print dresses of the other mothers. During this period of
social misprision, I made a trade with a girl from across the street of
a beautifully illustrated book of fairy tales for a comic book. When I
proudly showed my parents the comic book, they humiliatingly made
me go to the girl across the street and get the fairy-tale book back.
The parallel between my trade and the one they had made of Old
World culture for New World vitality was not apparent to them and
only now comes into view.

But I want to talk more about *skromnost*, about my family's practice
of it and my nostalgia for it. Today we recycle the things we don't want.
During my childhood and adolescence and young adulthood there
wasn't much we didn't want. It was a culture of conservation. And one
of being satisfied with what came our way. The way we live now would
have seemed unimaginably posh to middle-class people in the days
of millionaires rather than billionaires. Campbell's soup was not
associated with Andy Warhol. We ate it. Casseroles of noodles and
Campbell's cream-of-mushroom soup were a kind of national dish to
serve to company. Does anyone say 'casserole' anymore? Rich people
ate the cream-of-mushroom dishes along with the rest of us; I've
heard of rich old people whose servants still know how to make them.
Today, the non-poor eat exquisite food as a matter of course, and
four-year-old girls are taken for pedicures. This will be hard for young
people today to believe, but no one went for pedicures when I was
young. Sometimes for a very special occasion (the end of the world)

one had a manicure. It was administered at the hairdresser's while you were under the dryer.

I think of the *skromný* vacations we went on with our parents, in the time between the end of camp and the beginning of school. For several years, we stayed at the Andrews farm, in Pownal, Vermont, which took guests during the summer months, and served wonderful food: corn on the cob, cucumbers and green beans and tomatoes and potatoes from the garden, pork chops and steaks and chicken cutlets from their own or neighbors' animals – what we now call 'artisanal' food. We understood its rare deliciousness. It made up for the monotony of the place. Except for one activity, croquet, I don't know what we did all day. There was a girl named Gwendolyn who cheated at the game: she was always moving her ball or yours. In the evenings we and the four or five other families or couples staying at the farm gathered in the parlor. We played word games or Gwendolyn played the piano. She was pretty in a blond, sugary way. She played well. Marie and I hated her.

There were other summers when my mother couldn't get away from work and my father took us to New Hampshire, to stay in a roadside cabin, one of about eight, owned by a Mr Hitchcock. Again, I don't remember much about what we did – I think we toured New Hampshire places of interest like the Flume Gorge and Mt Washington, perhaps we swam in a nearby lake – but I remember the restaurant in a clapboard house across the road from our cabin, a little downhill, that served carefully prepared New England food and gave a special shine to the vacations. We ate breakfast and dinner there and felt fortunate. Here and there you still see collections of cabins on New England roads – I have passed one called Hubby's Cabins, near Great Barrington, Massachusetts – and I think of Mr Hitchcock and those blurred innocent vacations with my father.

Mother

She had an enormous amount of what used to be called 'European charm'. My sister and I, each in our way, acquired some of it from her. What is it? From the point of view of feminism, it seems kind of awful, not 'enabling' or enabling in the wrong way, the way the first wife in a harem might establish her firstness. By being charming you are lowering yourself. You are asking for something. I admire the deadpan young women of today who want nothing from you. I like their toughness and self-containment. Of course, beneath the surface, they are as pathetic as everyone else. But the pose has something to be said for it. My mother wasn't charming in a fluttering feminine way. She was sturdily built and had an affect of enthusiasm and vitality. But she belonged to her time, and this was a time when women worshipped men without ever quite coming out and saying so. It has taken me a long time to understand the implications of her legacy of charm.

My mother was not a 'good enough mother', as the psychoanalyst Donald Winnicott put it. She was a good mother. She was warm and loving and unselfish. I remember the incongruously delicious food she made for us when we were ill. One associates gruel and weak tea with illness. My mother made us roast squab and, unbelievably, profiteroles. This may be because she knew we were only malingering; we were allowed to call ourselves ill when the mercury thermometer reached what we called the *křížek* – the line marking the border between normal and elevated temperatures. The border was good enough. When we reached it, we could lie back on our pillows as the phone call to school was made.

My mother had a large nature, but I realize that my idea of it is vague and unformed. As I try to portray her I come up against what must be a strong resistance to doing so. Let me go back to the charm. Charmers want to know about you, they ask questions, they are so interested. You are flattered and warmed. Sometimes you grow flushed with the pleasure of the attention. I have seen people grow flushed while talking to me. Did I become a journalist because of knowing how to imitate my mother? When I ask someone a question – either in life or in work – I often don't listen to the answer. I am not really interested.[2] I don't think my mother was interested in what people told her, either. She asked her questions. But her mind was elsewhere. This is what I can't get hold of. What was she interested in? She was a reader. It was always an article of faith that she, and not my father, was the one who knew what great literature was, that she could always recognize the real thing, that hers was a kind of perfect pitch, while his taste was more commonplace, though he was the literary one, the one who wrote.

Her exuberance and vivacity and warmth were a kind of front for an inner deadness of spirit. She would put herself down. She would say she didn't do anything properly. It's *šmejd*, rubbish, she would say about what she did.

I realized later in life that she always had something the matter with her. We all have something the matter with us – go to any drugstore and you'll see that – but she seemed to suffer more than

---

[2] The use of a tape recorder during interviews permits me to counteract this obvious disqualification for my job. But, thinking about it further, I wonder whether a lot more of us, perhaps most of us, only pretend to be interested in the answers to the questions we ask, and whether the word 'empathy' refers to a performance rather than to a feeling.

most from the common minor ailments: muscle pain, indigestion, constipation, headache. At some point during my childhood there was talk about depression and about visits to a Dr Levine, a colleague of my father's. I have a letter from my father written when I was in college, entreating me to write to her more frequently, and saying that she was depressed and felt wounded by my carelessness and callousness. I also have a letter from her written just after putting me on the train for college, telling me how much she loved and admired me.

Sept. 15, 51

Darling Janet,

I started to write you a letter just after I returned from the station – it was a tearful letter and disgustingly sentimental. Now, I came back to my senses and I realize how good it is for you to be in a new atmosphere of such a great university. Of course I miss you and somehow I feel that I didn't tell you all the things I wanted. Not advices – I am so sure of you – I am very much handicapped by my poor English – but believe me I have not words even in Czech – to tell you how much I love you and how proud I am of you. You probably have realized that my relationship to you was not entirely the one of a mother towards the daughter, but many times just the other way. I have found in you all the traits of both my parents which I admired and loved so much.

I hope you had a good start and I wish you all the luck. Yesterday – Sunday – we were at the Traubs' cottage – it was a perfect day – lovely swimming and delicious steak dinner. Today back to work and this time I sort of looked forward to it.

So far I found only the brush you forgot and the nylon pants. I also bought a shoe bag for you and I am going to send it very soon.

I expect a letter from you tomorrow – but I want you to know that I will be quite patient and won't worry if your letters won't be on the dot. I also would like if you would write about the things you don't like just as about those you like – because this way we will stay sort of closer, don't you think so?

Drahoušku, moc Tě miluji a stále na tebe myslím.

Líbam Tě tvá máma.

[Darling, I love you very much and think about you all the time. Your mother kisses you.]

'I expect a letter from you tomorrow.' Did it come? Did I write it? Here is what my father wrote in a letter a year and a half later:

Darling, although we love one another in our family as much and as deeply as in any other family/ we may consider our family as an emotional and intellectual success/, you know that Joan needs more overt display of genuine emotions and more affectionate climate than we all other together. We all probably are in our innermost core the same or almost the same but we all sort of cover it by a shell of detachment and occasionally cynicism or something like that. Mother thrives only in this cornucopia of abundant warm emotions and we should give her as much of it as we can, since, if she does not get it, she is blaming herself and turning it against herself/ and particularly now, in her age, she has more tendency to this self-blame and self-depreciation and ensuing depression.

Darling, Joan is a wonderful person, since these qualities seem to be rare in this century. I am aware that I myself did not always satisfy these needs though I tried my best. I am sure we will all need her one day more than she needs us and we have to do everything to keep her in good spirits and happy. Please, darling, and you are a wonderful girl, too/, write Joan few lines/ non-Gargoylian, with the punch line: love, affection, appreciation, all those feelings you harbor a-plenty but do not express/. Darling, give it a thought. Maybe I am expressing my self in somewhat clumsy way but I am sure you will understand. There are times in our life when we need more emotional support and Joan is just now in such a period of life. Darling, Joan should not know that I wrote you this letter. I am sure you will find your way and form to dispel the clouds and doubts.

Non-Gargoylian. The *Gargoyle* was the college humor magazine I worked on, and in whose 'humorous' style my letters home were couched. My parents kept my letters and when I read them now I am ashamed and mortified. My mother wanted love and appreciation and I gave her stupid jokes. How could I have been so cruel and callow? But there may have been another pressure – the pressure to be funny – that was working on me and dictating my awful smart-ass letters. Our family was proud of the way we horsed around and had fun. The 'shell of detachment and cynicism' was a style we all liked and cultivated. My father was the dégagé cynic-in-chief, the most brilliantly humorous of us all, but my mother could be funny herself, perhaps more so in Czech than in English, but she was hardly the simple, warm, affection-starved woman he depicts in his letter. She participated in the family mockery of the Mr Collinses and Madame Verdurins who came our way. She didn't intercede for them; her desire for a 'cornucopia of warm emotions' didn't extend that far. I had gotten mixed signals, and I seem to have resolved the conflict by ignoring the demands it would have been harder to satisfy. The fear of speaking from the heart is deep-seated. We form the habit of defending ourselves against rejection early on. But, God, what a jerk I was. I can only blush with shame at those idiotic letters to my lovely mother. What would it have cost me to tell her that I loved her? But then I come across a letter that makes me side with myself against my mother:

> Last night she [my sister, then in high school] went square dancing and came home at 1:30. I was absolutely desperate – I don't think I was so scared in all my life. I did not know where she was or with whom – so I was just sitting and waiting and praying and crying. Then she came and was very upset to see me so upset. She simply forgot the time. I am still half dead today. Well, *c'est la vie*!

La vie with Mother's hysterical iron grip over her children's comings and goings wasn't easy. I remember having to leave parties to meet the curfew and sometimes finding her on the street in front of our building with a coat thrown over her nightgown. New York was fairly safe then – the crime period came later – and we traveled by bus and subway. We didn't drive. What was there to fear? I remember having to leave a party in the Bronx just when a boy I was interested in was beginning to seem interested in me. Flouting my mother's rule was out of the question. I never saw the boy again.

Many years later I won an award from a journalism school for a magazine piece about a family therapist, and I invited my father to the award ceremony. When my name was called, I got up and said thank you and sat down again. I didn't make the type of speech the other award winners had made. I thought those speeches were stupid and sentimental. I felt above them. I didn't realize how stupid and insufferable I myself was, how empty and embarrassing my gesture of purity was. My father said then and a few times afterwards that I should have made a speech like the others. One day he said this one time too many and I exploded at him. We were sitting around the table, at lunch. My explosion was followed instantly by an explosion from my mother. 'HOW DARE YOU SPEAK THAT WAY TO YOUR FATHER!!!' A flash of insight came to me. I saw my mother's all-powerful place in the family. The family therapist had spoken of a switchboard that powerful mothers manned. Everything that happened in the family had to go through them. Here was my mother enacting the metaphor. Yes, all happy families are alike in the pain their members helplessly inflict upon one another, as if under orders from a perverse higher authority.

More on Mother

I have been reading – not happily – letters that my mother wrote to me in the 1950s. I am pained by the 'Why haven't you written?' motif that runs through so many of them. I am pained both for her and for myself. It must have been bitter for me to be constantly reproached for my exercise of the prerogative of youth to be careless and selfish. But what I see now that I didn't see then is that her need for letters from me was a kind of sickness, like the sickness of being in love, and since I was in love all the time myself, I might have seen her as a fellow-sufferer rather than as an adversary whose thrusts I must parry to protect my wobbly independence.

My mother was temperamental. She was volatile, she could fly off the handle. We – my sister and I – knew this about her and didn't take it seriously; she was never unkind to us. She certainly never abused us. She just allowed herself her histrionics. One of the reproachful letters – 'It's two weeks since you wrote – thank god we have the *Daily* and found a story written by you. I don't see why you could not find 2 minutes to write home' – ends with the outburst, 'I am too mad to write more.' In another letter – for once not on the why-don't-you-write theme – she tells of a lucrative job offer at Radio Free Europe she turned down and lashes out: 'Everybody thinks I am an idiot – but I simply don't feel like working and nobody can force me.'

I remember a scene in which she packed a suitcase and said she was leaving. She had had enough. In the scene, Marie and I and my father are watching her pack the suitcase. She seemed to mean it, but

I don't remember any feeling of distress. I think we all knew that this was farce of some kind. Of course she didn't leave.

I think the issue was my grandmother, my father's mother, who lived with us. Something about the threads and pins from her sewing that were always all over the floor. My grandmother was a kindly, well-meaning woman who was a great trial to my mother. It is rare for wives to happily welcome their mothers-in-law into their households, but this mother-in-law must have been particularly hard to live with precisely because of her harmlessness and kindliness – and depression. In a document titled 'My Confession', Babička, as we called my grandmother, writes of her miserable childhood as the unloved thirteenth child of parents who sent her to live with a married sister, who mistreated her. The grim childhood ended with a loveless arranged marriage that ended in divorce when my father was an infant. Babička's 'Confession' puts me in mind of Chekhov's stories about brutal peasant life and of his spare recollections of his own childhood as the son of a serf who caused him to wonder every day whether he would be beaten. Somewhere Chekhov wrote about having to squeeze the serf out of himself. I have wondered how my father squeezed the serf out of himself, my witty, erudite, kind, unselfish, gentle father. The vestiges of his peasant childhood – his personal parsimony (he was generous toward others), some kind of lack of Hapsburg polish that annoyed my mother – were insignificant, though my sister and I may have sided with my mother in the airs she put on. We always knew he came from a village and she from a Prague apartment with art nouveau wallpaper.

I don't want to exaggerate my mother's attachment to refinement. She had an earthiness of her own that her temperament and temper expressed, and she was never cruel to my grandmother. She just got fed up from time to time. We all felt guilty about my grandmother. I learned only later that she was clinically depressed and received shock treatments, and that they helped. I don't know where she received the treatments. It could not have been in my father's office at our apartment, where – yes, this is true – my father (assisted by my mother) gave shock treatments to some of his patients. This was actually allowed in the 1940s. ∎

ADAM CVIJANOVIC
Surrender at Appomattox, 2021

TALK AMERICA

George Prochnik

B y the time I left Jerusalem at the end of the 1990s, I'd run out
of cash and seen my personal debt ceiling collapse. For years
I'd gotten by with piecework verbal peddling, teaching in different
capacities and writing occasional pieces of cultural journalism. Only I
hadn't really gotten by, since I kept having to borrow to survive, and so
kept falling further behind. One of the understandings I reached with
my family about coming back to America was that I would henceforth
give up the aspiration that the writing I so cared about could support me
economically, and would set about finding a 'real job' – something I'd
managed to avoid doing well into my thirties, even if I did continually
labor at a motley array of not-real jobs.

Of course, I dreaded the prospect. But I was also sick to death
of scrounging, and confronting the reality over and over that what I
earned didn't quite add up to what I needed for rent, food and so on.
I'd had enough of beating my brains out trying to solve the puzzle of
how to earn a living without compromising my values or exhausting
my energies for writing creatively. I had young children. It was time to
act like a grown-up, even though I'd never really bought into the idea
that maturity and regular, salaried employment were synonymous.

Nonetheless, I would get a full-time job, and I'd write what I
liked in the interstices, the way other artistic people did when they

took their real-world responsibilities seriously. What exactly would I do? Well, it seemed clear to me I'd find work writing for somebody else. Some person or entity with a bank account. Working every day for a newspaper or magazine, presumably, or perhaps with a book publisher.

Several months after returning, having fruitlessly pursued countless leads in publishing and at not-for-profits, I was still unemployed. Without retracing the long, painful convolutions of my efforts to find work, I will say only that at the end of the fall I finally ended up being hired for $8.50 an hour by the customer service call center of Talk America: an infomercial marketer of products like Protein Power Package and of supplements for reversing the effects of male pattern baldness – of colon cleansers, brain builders, miracle diets, youth restorers, romance finders, moneymakers and other all-around fate transformers. Talk America! And *tickety-tock*, America talked to me. I sat in Portland, Maine, at a tiny desk in a big fluorescent crossword puzzle of a room, taking call after call after call, the script for most of which went something like this:

'Hi, this is George at Talk America, how can I help you today?'

'You *fucking* liars! I got your Super Body Ultra Reboot machine and it's just a bunch of fucking broken plastic and springs with a bullshit video of some asshole lifting shit!'

'I'm very sorry if you're disappointed with the product, sir. It's been endorsed as you know by many of the world's top super body –'

'You get my money back overnight or you'll be sorry mother*fucker* –'

'We're happy to refund you your money, sir, if you're disappointed with our product, though we're very sorry to hear it. Are you sure you practiced the technique exactly as Buddy Beef Bronzer the Human Muscle Dump demonstrates?'

(Inchoate, gore-spattered screaming.)

'Okay, well then, we can get the refund process started right away upon receipt of the merchandise, sir. It usually takes a few weeks until the next check printing, but –'

'YOU GET ME my FUCKING *money* tomorrow *morning*!'

'We're happy to provide you with a full refund just as soon as we receive back the super-builder product, at which point the refund can be processed – minus the $19.95 shipping and handling fee from our end . . .'

That was the point in the narrative at which I winced and braced, the part that always spelled the start of real trouble. It was when the person whose body had not undergone an Olympian reinvigoration in a few weeks – whose brain had not yet hit trans-Einstein levels, who was still getting older, heavier, more drained, flaccid, broke, bald, clogged and isolated – learned that the shipping and handling fees, on a box of junky bits one might feel annoyed by if it came as a bonus gift with a piece of gum from a vending machine, cost practically as much as the product itself, that conversation broke down altogether.

'You know what I'm doing right now?'

'No sir. Shall I indicate then that we should be expecting the return of your –'

'I'm loading my guns in the back of my truck. I'm going to start driving tonight. I'll be at your *fucking* offices in fourteen hours and I'll blow all y'all's fucking heads off.'

'I'm sorry you're disappointed with the product, sir.'

'Blow your *fucking* brains out! All over the walls! You cocksucking, motherfuh—'

Well, it made a change from teaching Keats and Shakespeare to gifted, eager classes of Israeli and Palestinian students at the Hebrew University of Jerusalem.

I know the call sounds exaggerated, but I swear I received death threats in language almost identical to what I've just transcribed. And even short of people saying they would kill me, which did happen – twice – the rage and despair I listened to each day was monumental. I never questioned people's right to a refund. I never said much beyond vowing that I would do everything I could to expedite their refund, trying to calm them down, and then taking off my headset, leaving my desk, and begging my superiors to help the worst victims. Far more upsetting than the murderous dupes were the people who just broke down sobbing at the failure of their Talk America product, as seen on TV, to have redeemed one single aspect of their tragic existence.

God, the endless lost tribes of consumers that the Talk America sales team managed to seduce. The *hope* they tapped into and turned into credit-card number read-alouds over the phone. The *faith* of those poor souls all over the country. On the rare occasions when someone sounded a little less desperate, I'd try to engage them in conversation, to gain some understanding of their larger experience. The experience, time and again, of failure, poverty, wrenching struggle and betrayal, tacked onto the dream that a Talk America bauble would make their lives great again for the first time ever. Thinking back now on the hundreds of conversations I had at the center, how could I have been surprised for an instant by the possibility of Trump's election? He was like every Talk America product rolled up together in a single throbbing flesh totem. Trump was Talk America in commander-in-chief form.

But at last my Talk America education came to an end. In late winter, a friend in New York called to say that someone he knew who worked at a public relations firm in Midtown was looking for a writer and he'd given the guy my contact information. Shortly thereafter I found myself entering a black office building on the Avenue of the Americas that looked like a coffin of the gods slipped down from the clouds. I walked out of the elevator into a quiet reception room on the forty-second floor. I walked from office to office, greeting different executives whose long glass windows presided over the dormant trees in Central Park, or across a panoply of skyscrapers resembling fossilized organ pipes.

Of course, I took the job. Sixty thousand dollars a year and health insurance half paid by the company? I'd never made anything near that. I felt like a plutocrat. I did manage to continually work on my own books while hiding in my cubicle in that office. I did try to subvert almost everything I wrote, living by the principle 'bite the hand that feeds you' – slipping in quotes from Dostoevsky and Tarkovsky in a stump speech I wrote for the Duchess of York; weaving seditious political references through long, dry business documents. But notwithstanding the ways I tried to undermine what I was doing I was still with the firm almost two decades later. (In Žižek's words, 'Even if we do not take things seriously . . . *we are still doing them.*') What I'd thought would be a matter of a few years, long enough that I could crawl out of debt and find some more noble, decently paid work, turned into something closer to a life sentence. And each year the comfort of having my core expenses paid by the company became harder to dispense with, while those expenses slowly crept up. I was still working there, selling verbal snake oil to whomever would pay.

Sometimes I would try to console myself with the thought that most of the copy I wrote was for not-for-profits – hospitals, addiction-recovery centers, scientific research institutes, children's aid funds and so on. But of course the truth was that this made the work more despicable. There was no reason to believe that a rehab facility that could afford to pay for a Midtown public relations program was any better than the facility that didn't have such a budget for self-promotion. It was a completely arbitrary elevation of non-profit newsworthiness on the basis of money-raising prowess. As for the dozens of assignments I had with the philanthropic divisions of various large companies, I cannot think today of a single instance when the business agenda didn't ultimately poison and warp the project it supported. When it comes to corporate sponsors, there is no such thing as a benign public-private partnership. The public interest is always mutilated to make it fit the firm's bottom-line goals, a systemic version of the vicious custom of foot binding.

And anyway, it wasn't true. Most of what I was writing by 2016 consisted of new business proposals for potential real estate clients, explaining how the agency would place positive stories about their buildings in outlets monitored by potential buyers, investors and brokers, along with larger 'thought pieces' detailing the rejuvenating, dynamizing neighborhood impact these developments would have, aimed at local community boards and decision makers. It was pure chance that I never wrote anything for the Trump Organization itself.

If I paid my debt for having so debased myself by losing a significant part of my time on Earth to that labor, I yet excuse none of it. Not a day. Not a ghostwritten speech for the head of a single environmental initiative. Not a sentence. Not a word. Not a syllable. Why should my language have come from that woman or man's mouth at the rate of God-knows-what a minute? It was all lies and deceit. I allowed myself to become the voice of people I despised, or who had money enough not to have to speak for themselves. I sold the aspect of myself I cared for most deeply.

People talk frequently, often self-flagellatingly, about 'bubbles' and 'silos' in the attempt to analyze why educated East Coast liberals had no idea what was coming in November 2016. *We were locked inside our precious little self-affirming feeds and mutually reinforcing insular exchanges,* runs the narrative. But I reject this diagnosis. Whether through conversation with friends who had loved ones in areas that did vote for Trump, with people in the flag-waving suburb where I'd gone to high school, or my time at Talk America, or the grassroots reporting that did emerge from parts of the country left behind by the tides of globalization, I knew something about the resentment people felt elsewhere, and about the vulnerability to populist politics this sense of grievance engendered, even if I didn't register the level of vengeful elation-in-waiting.

Whenever one rides the subway, as I did every weekday for almost twenty years, one bursts the bubble of one's private existence and encounters a deeply heterogeneous array of humanity and socioeconomic circumstances. A single walk down a New York City street can enlarge perspectives and pop the self-reinforcing narrative of anyone with their eyes open. People living in more narrowly patriotic communities where Fox News or the like is playing constantly in public spaces will be more susceptible to siloed viewpoints than someone navigating the urban commons. I was not in a bubble, but in a way my position was more culpable: with all my ideals, my sympathies, my higher literary, philosophical and artistic fascinations, I'd found no means of supporting myself except as a parasite in the belly of the same system where the monster of the deal had incubated. The reason that I hadn't foreseen the results of the election wasn't that I was locked away, blinds drawn, with my cortado coffee and Roland Barthes; it was because I couldn't face the implications of my own participation in the system the president epitomized and sought to impose on creation. If there were bubbles involved, I was inside Trump's golden belch. And when I looked around there, like Dorothy waking from her dream of Oz, I recognized almost everyone I knew, hovering beside me. ∎

Payne Whitney Psychiatric Clinic, New York Hospital, New York, USA
Courtesy of the Library of Congress

THE MOVING TARGET OF BEING

Suzanne Scanlon

(*Return*)

It was a hot day in July, the summer of 2015, and I happened to be in New York. I was house-sitting for a friend, spending a week in her apartment at 145th and Broadway. It was the closest I'd been in years to the hospital that had once been my home. One morning, I decided to walk north. My best days are those that I walk the city, unfettered and directionless, and so it took me a minute to understand where I was going. We are drawn back, aren't we? Even when we don't mean to be and don't want to be. The past is there, waiting for us. I walked the mile or so up Riverside Drive, until I reached my one-time address: 722 W 168th Street.

Of course nothing in this city remains as it was, and this is no exception: the building, with its grand architecture, is no longer the home of the State Psychiatric Institute. Now it is the School of Public Health.

This is where I lived, I want to say to someone, as I point up to the fifth floor. But who would care?

In the archway over the entrance, I can read the original name of the building, the Romanesque lettering etched in stone: NEW YORK

STATE PSYCHIATRIC INSTITUTE + HOSPITAL. It is a vestige, for which I am grateful. I look for another: the benches out front. One stone bench etched with the Roman numeral MDCCXCV, the year of the building's founding. But it's not there.

*

Just a year or so after I left for good, the State Psychiatric Institute moved into a new building, larger and grander than the original, with a walkway crossing Riverside Drive toward a second building, which looked out to the Hudson River. By then the program was defunded. No longer would anyone live there as we did.

I find the department of records. I ask a woman at the desk about the old building, the state hospital connected with the Presbyterians of Columbia University, the institute referred to as PI. She looks at me flatly, uninterested. Yes, she says. That's the 'old PI'.

I tell her I'd like to get copies of my medical records.

Were you an inpatient?

Yes.

When?

A long time ago.

How long ago?

Twenty years ago, I realize as I say it.

She considers, then explains the process of retrieving records. There are forms to fill out, fees to pay, permissions for release. Once this is approved, the papers will be copied. You'll receive those copies in the mail.

I fill out the paperwork. I pay with my credit card.

It's nearly a year later, I've almost forgotten, when I receive a packet of ten or fifteen pages. A summary of my stay. A stack of narratives, really. Different doctors write different summaries. Each doctor has his or her particular angle. Did I think it would be objective? No, but I hadn't realized how subjective it would be. These character descriptions have much in common with the work of the students in my creative-writing classes. There are consistencies, recurring themes: dysthymia is used over and over again. I was told I had chronic depression, or major depression, or bipolar disorder, but dysthymia is the diagnosis that is repeated throughout the records.

I was disappointed by the stack of papers, which I put away in a drawer. On the one hand, these pages bring up the great shame I feel for the waste of those days, the extent of my abjection. At the same time, I wanted more – daily notes or details that could fill in the gaps in my notebooks, in my memory. I want the banal details. I don't want the official language, the axis one or axis two, the list of medications and symptoms. What I want is the story of our long, dull days and years in that hospital. Those days, those years. It is the quotidian I want to recover.

(*His Mother*)

Years after I was discharged, I found a photograph on the internet. It is a photograph of Allen Ginsberg from 1950, standing in front of that old building at 722 W 168th Street, near Riverside Drive. He's been a patient there for one year. In the photo he stands next to Marilyn Monroe, who stands next to Arthur Miller.

I don't know why I have such a clear memory of this photograph. I look for it now but can't find it. No matter, I still see it: Marilyn Monroe leans into Miller and looks away from the camera. Ginsberg stares straight into the camera's lens; a doctor stands on the other side of Monroe.

And one more trick of memory. I see now that the man standing next to Marilyn Monroe is Joe DiMaggio, not Arthur Miller. How I recognize him as DiMaggio I'm not certain, but I know that it is a husband who escorts her; I also know that it doesn't matter much which – either one is viable in this photograph.

Anyway, I don't want to talk about Allen Ginsberg, though he did dedicate *Howl* to Carl Solomon, the friend he met in that hospital.

A friend who got shocks and a straitjacket. The way he and Solomon tried to decide if they were crazy or the doctors were crazy.

And he said something about leaving the hospital, about the self rejection, the way you've internalized all that you've been told is wrong with you; how you bring that out into the world with you. How he walked the streets after discharge, seeking validation everywhere, not finding it. How he had to get out of New York.

And if I say anything about Ginsberg and madness, I should say something about his mother, Naomi Ginsberg, whose story didn't just begin in an institution but ended there, too. Naomi Ginsberg who was institutionalized, who was lobotomized, who died in a state hospital. If her son was the exception, the young man whose year inside led to the richness of a long life in literature, then she was the rule.

(*Where It Began*)

I arrived in January of 1992. New York City: all darkness and disinterest. Who the fuck cared that you arrived? Millions arrived here every day. The streets around the campus were empty, save for passing traffic, buses, the occasional bodega. Empty styrofoam cups, plastic tops, straws and McDonald's bags floated in a wet slushy bath of ice. Piles of dog shit half frozen under the snow. A security guard informed me that my dorm was a few blocks away, on the other side of campus. I walked the long blocks, dragging a duffel bag.

My room was one in a suite, with a shared kitchen and bathroom. The floors were cold tile; the walls concrete; the only furnishings a metal twin bed, a desk and a small window with a view of a brick wall.

I dropped my bags, locked the door and walked to the deli next door.

When I returned, my suite mates were there, a triptych of young womanhood.

Hello, I said, stabbing a baked potato twice before putting it in the microwave.

Is that all you're eating? a small chatty girl asked, giggling. I felt my body flood, and knew I'd turned bright red.

Yes, I said. I guess so.

A month later and I haven't made a single friend. You can become strange from loneliness, from days and weeks without speaking to anyone. Occasionally someone from home will call, and I'll pretend everything is fine. In my notebook, I chronicle my despair. Today is Valentine's Day and David is coming into town. He asks me to meet him downtown.

On the train, I stand across from a stranger. We are close enough to make out, my face in his, but here's the rule: no eye contact. Pretend you are not this close to someone's humanity. Look away or at your feet but never at a face. Get off at Christopher Street, David had said. I hold my laminated *Streetwise Manhattan* like a prayer card. The train screeches and jerks out of the station. I smell urine and ham, rat shit and perfume. When I close my eyes I see the chickens again, dangling from their feet, moving toward me. I hear a woman cry. The train stops and starts again and again with a jerk, 72nd, 66th, my head against the green doors, red paint splattered across each, as if someone took a giant Sharpie to it. A scene from a movie: *Six Weeks*, the young sick ballerina collapsing on a New York subway, all possibility, all devastation.

Another train passes and I read the graffiti, big white bubble letters jumping out like demented ghosts, the words: ONE IS YOU and IS BACK legible in the splatter. ONE IS YOU: I hear it over and over again, my head softly leaning against the train door. An announcement for Times Square. From one window faces speed past, and from the other more graffiti. The man next to me is only mildly threatening, in that serial killer way.

Excuse me, I ask.

He turns to look down at me, I see his sharply cut jaw.

Have we passed Christopher Street?

The train stopped so many times. How could I know?

He's annoyed. Yes, yes I am a Midwestern idiot. No, I don't know what I am doing here.

Look. He points to the map on the side of the train car. Now he looks me up and down, stopping at my breasts. I pull my coat tight.

23rd Street. A few more to go.

D avid is seated, holding the menu and shaking his leg below the table. *Where were you?* he hisses. This neighborhood is another world entirely. A few weeks in the city and it's my first time leaving the environs of campus, from 116th to 120th, from Riverside Drive to Amsterdam Avenue. There was a darkness to the village, to every street. Peep shows. This was New York before the real estate investment, before Giuliani decided to sell it, to market it, before Giuliani *cleaned up* Times Square. This was the time of Aids, men were dying all around us, but we didn't know. Alphabet City, which would later reach iconic status via *Rent*, then full of abandoned buildings, garbage floating in the water on the curb. Kathy Acker lived there, though we didn't know. It would be a year or two before I read the way she channeled madness into artistic practice, and found the space she would open for me. Writing is like suicide, she wrote, only you don't have to die.

David didn't get up. I sat and he asked again what took me so long. I was overwhelmed by the gap between what I'd imagined for months, the possibility of a true connection with this man, and how I loved him. And now here he was and we were as far apart as two people could be. I heard it again: ONE IS YOU. Now David is saying something I can't understand; his face floating over the table like a fat balloon. IS BACK. That gauzy feeling, a trap: everything could get in, no boundary between my body and the rest.

Suzy? The balloon is saying something. What was this city, another planet, a nightmare. I told IS BACK to shut up, I told myself: the balloon is real. This is real, I said. I am in New York. I am with the man I met a year ago in Los Angeles, a foreign country. Every choice that led me here, to this place, to this moment, was now revealed to be absurd, utterly random. I had told myself it was my choice, but maybe I did just follow David here. And now here we were but we weren't here. I couldn't follow him, how stupid to think so.

Sorry, I said. I apologized for everything, that way of young women.

I'm really sorry I'm so late. I had trouble figuring out the train.

I didn't tell him that I'd gotten lost coming out of the Christopher Street stop. Every street became something else, circles into circles. My *Streetwise* didn't help.

Well let's order. I'm starving! Anyway, why are you so thin?

I mean, I'm into it, he added. It's your Jane Austen look. It's nice! It's good, I like it.

I read the menu. I'd never had Indian food.

Do you like dal? We should get naan with mango chutney, okay? You'll love it, I promise. I'll order.

The food arrived: a feast of naan, dal, curries and biryani; David ate quickly, talking while he ate, talking in between large bites, all the while explaining what he was doing at Sarah Lawrence, directing a stage adaptation of Bergman's *Persona*. It wasn't going well. The actors didn't understand the tone. It was going to be a failure, he was sure of it.

Why aren't you eating? He finally noticed.

I took a few bites. I tried the chutney on the bread and it was delicious, flavors I'd never tasted.

The waiter came back, asked how it was.

I can't eat this, I said, pointing to the food in front of me.

Why not?

There's oil in it.

Oil?

I leaned toward David and whispered: There are things in it. I've read about it.

David laughed, then looked at me like I was crazy. The waiter nodded and said he would see what he could do.

You're insane! Who doesn't eat OIL?

I watched David eat, samosa after samosa. I listened to his loud smacking noises, watched him shove the food down, as if in a competition.

Do you want a beer?

No, I said. I don't drink. I've been reading a lot about all the poisons in food and alcohol. There's a lot you don't know. I'm trying to purify.

The waiter never returned. I would go home hungry that night, but it was better that way. David moved to say goodbye, a kiss on the cheek. My hair stayed in my face and I held my arms tight.

On the subway, I opened *As I Lay Dying*. The body as meat. The mother's body is meat. I read the same page over and over again. *That was when I learned that words are no good; that words don't ever fit even what they are trying to say at.* I heard voices, saw people, friends and family, my mother. Say it. *My mother is a fish.* Say it, this trap, I see it now, my life.

The next day I went to the student health center in the basement of campus, winding through tunnels to find the office. I spoke to a nurse. I explained what was happening: my hair, the poisons, the voices, the visions. The nurse said, You need to see the doctor. Dr Goldberg. She asked me to explain. I don't know what I said. I do remember she was the first to ask me this question, the first person besides David to use the words in conversation (it wasn't like now, with the word, the idea, the act all over the internet – back then, few people spoke of it). Dr Goldberg asked me: Do you want to kill yourself? Or did she say, Do you want to hurt yourself? Or, Do you have thoughts of hurting yourself or someone else? Or, Do you want to commit suicide? Was that it?

Whatever it was, I said yes. It was true, and no one but David had asked. Yes, I said. I think about it all the time.

It began there, that yes, saying yes out loud to a person who seemed to care – and that first yes became an opening, the word a possibility.

She said, I'm going to give you a prescription. I want to see you in a week.

I don't think I'd heard of Prozac before, it was still so new. There was nothing like the so-called direct-to-consumer advertising we're so used to now. A few years later there would be books: Peter D. Kramer's *Listening to Prozac* and Elizabeth Wurtzel's *Prozac Nation*. And soon after, those creepy commercials. Ask your doctor if Zoloft might be right for you. Etc.

Yes, that's where it began: that question. That prescription. The next day, or two or three days, when I didn't sleep. I could stick with the program. The program enlarged, more to do, more hours of walking through the city, the sense of possibility.

Then one day I went to class, Death in Modern Fiction, and I heard a girl say, If you go to the health center and tell them you're sad or whatever, they'll give you Prozac. If you say you broke up with your boyfriend, they'll give you Prozac. Everyone around her laughed. She was so cool, sophisticated in that raised-in-Manhattan way so foreign to me. They hand it out like candy, she said.

She was talking about me. I knew it. Now I knew that it meant nothing, that the doctor didn't know me, she knew Prozac. It was just one more poison.

I stopped taking the pills. I was done.

But nothing stopped. Everything was so bright.

David and I spoke by phone, often for hours at a time. We spoke of suicide as a matter of course. It was what we needed to do. He grew up in the city, he'd been in analysis since high school. He hated the analyst, didn't trust him. He had been through the whole system. All the psychiatrists suck, he told me, never trust them.

Let's just do it, he would say, before hanging up. I'd agree. Of course, I said. We have to. I want to.

When I read the official medical records, I see that this is where the story begins. No matter what, you need a beginning. And this became mine. The narrative over and over again in these pages: the night David called me. I was at my desk studying for midterms. Reading my notes. David called, he was upset, he said he couldn't take it anymore, it was something about his dad, his play. He was in his car, he said, the college had forced him to see a disgusting psychiatrist and he'd been saving up the pills. He stole a few bottles from his mother's bathroom. He had enough for both of us. You want to do it, right? he asked me. I'm coming to get you now. We'll take all of the pills. I had two bottles. We have enough, he said. I wasn't sure. I have to study, I said. Nothing's going to change, he said. You know that right? It's all the same. It doesn't matter if you study.

I said no, I can't, maybe tomorrow I'll do it. Not now, I said. He hung up on me.

And the day after that phone call, when I didn't hear from David. When he didn't answer the phone, when his roommate said no one had seen him in days, when his mother said he was at school as far as she knew, when I became sure that he was dead.

And the next day, after the exam, after I spent those hours writing in my blue books. It began when I left class, and it became clear. The screw. The faces. I knew I was shut out and it would always be this way. I would never be close to anyone and I would live in this trap for the rest of my life. David was right.

I went back to my desk that afternoon and took out the pills, two bottles, lining them up in a row, one after another – green and orange capsules stamped E 92. It meant something. Yes, I said. The space opened, the Yes.

It was as easy as this, a breaking down of all boundaries, it was David who showed me. I felt happy.

The desk was long and wooden, with a laminated plastic covering and metal legs. My books sat there, a presence. The screw. I couldn't keep up with the program. It was there when I woke, the imperatives: do this and this then this and this do not stop you suck you will fail you are ugly you have so much to learn you are so far behind you will never succeed you will always be alone your loneliness will never be rocked you will never write the way your heroes do.

I imagined David counting the pills and I could do this too, one after the other, a row or two rows, a line or two lines, counting and it would be enough, I swallowed each row, one and another, stuffing my mouth full, swallowing until I choked. I sipped from my water bottle and lay on my bed: metal frame, thin mattress, one blanket, a crunchy pillow. I waited. I saw the faces on my wall. I could hear one or the other laughing. I heard Leonard Lopate's voice on the radio. The window. The brick wall. I couldn't see out but it all got in: the incessant sounds of that city: an ambulance, birds screeching, garbage trucks, shouting, car horns. I was going to vomit, I was too awake it was all taking too long. I turned into a fetal position. A loneliness that can be rocked. The great female tragedy. My mother my love. It was too late. I ate books, I could live here.

(*The New York State Psychiatric Institute*)

I was led onto the elevator by a nurse. I was brought to an office. This was August, 1992. I took off my shoelaces and handed over sharps: my eyeliner, pencil sharpener, a compact mirror, a spiral notebook. I met a doctor. He may or may not have asked questions. He said it would be six months. Wasn't it three? I asked. He nodded. We'll see, he said, it usually takes longer than that. I signed papers, I agreed to something. They were not forcing me to be there, not really, though what else would I have done? If I say now: that was the moment – I should have said no thank you, I should have walked out – it wouldn't mean anything to the person I was then. She could not imagine leaving, she could not imagine being anywhere else.

By then I had been in the hospital for months, since that night in March. They needed me to get better and instead I got better at being sick. I got better at being a mental patient. I got better at planning my death and better at speaking to psychiatrists.

Others in the short-term ward would come and go, most older than me. They'll keep you thirty days or until your insurance runs out, one or another would say. Then you're cured.

It was a joke. The system was rigged and they told me so.

Still, I believed in it. It was saving me. I was lucky. I was on student insurance until I dropped out of school, and by then I was in a state hospital. Everything was free. I did not have to leave.

You sit in an office until a nurse comes to tell you, We have a bed. You walk down a hallway, pass a kitchen, a service elevator, more offices. Locked doors, vinyl couches, a television. Now your room, a bed, no door. One window of laminated glass, unbreakable. A chair. Metal bars behind the plastic. Your room. You have a bag of clothes and a bag of books. You see into the room of the girl across the hall, pink and purple bedding and stuffed animals, a poster from an Anne Rice movie. Clothes on the floor, books. She doesn't look at you, doesn't say hi.

I fall asleep there, thin sheets pulled over me. Sheets marked with a stamp: PROPERTY OF THE NEW YORK STATE PSYCHIATRIC INSTITUTE. Whatever they gave me – clozapine, thorazine – has made me dizzy and sick. A nurse named Nevada walks down the hall, knocking on the wall where the door would be. Dinner! she repeats over and over, cheery robotic, too loud. It's dark out. I don't know what day it is, and soon enough it will mean little, days and time itself become insignificant. I have to hold the wall, walking to the dining area. Dinner trays stacked on the shelves of a silver cart.

Take one! Nevada calls from behind me. We don't serve you here!

I take my tray and walk into the shared dining room. I can feel the cold concrete through my hospital socks. Rows of tables. A view of the Hudson River. At the back corner table I see a woman, older than the rest. She wears a long dress, unlike the others in hospital gowns or scrubs. The dress is lace, a threadbare Laura Ashley dyed black, fishnet tights and jewelry: bracelets, earrings, long beaded necklaces. When I sit alone at a table, she is the first one to greet me. Hello, she says, my name is Jennifer. Hi, I say. She looks at my tray: a scoop of mashed potatoes, slices of beef, green peas and a roll. A cup of pudding on the side. You don't have to eat it, you know. I wasn't planning to. Well, I get people to bring me food. You can do that, you know? There's a refrigerator here, if you want, my husband can get you something, I'll tell him. Whatever you need. I thanked her. Well. When you're done eating or getting settled in you should come back and see my table. My jewelry table. I see the assortment of beads, stones, jewelry cutters. Now I notice the woman next to Jennifer, standing near, walking where she walks, always by her side, close enough to hold her.

Now a nurse named Maxine walks into the room, calls me by my full name: Suzanne. She holds a Dixie Cup filled with more pills. Suzanne? She looks around, then at me. Are you Suzanne? I say no, I'm Suzy. She replies, It says here your name is Suzanne. I say yes, but no one calls me that. It's your name, she says, flatly. I'm not going to call you Suzy. That's a cheerleader name.

The next day she'll call me Suzanne and I won't correct her. I know what your problem is, she'll say, you think you are special. Look around you. She makes a grand sweeping gesture indicating all the sad young women in the dining room. Everyone here thinks she is special.

I make a call back home on the payphone. Get me out of this place, I say to my father, my sister. But of course it is too late. You are not ready, they tell me. You are very sick. It will take time. It gets worse before it gets better.

I lived in that hospital for three years. When I think of the other women in the hospital, I don't think of madness, or insanity, I don't even think of mental illness, though of course it was there, it was the story we were told and we were learning to tell about ourselves. Instead, I think of mothers. Some of these women were mothers;

some had a mother; some had lost a mother. I watched these women closely, hungry to understand what I did not have.

(*Another Hospital*)

I'm eight years old. My third-grade teacher tells me that she'll be bringing me to the hospital after school. I love third grade: equations and parts of speech, affixes and prefixes. I love Shel Silverstein's 'Sick'. I love sitting in my own triangle pod with two boys named Eric Twitt and Brian Salerno. I like my teacher, Mrs Achim, with her smoker's cough and side-eye; I like my distance from her, too. I like that she stands at the front of the classroom and that we sit in seats about the room. I like that I can be one of the crowd, not really an I.

Mrs Achim is my mom's friend. My mom had many friends. I can see them now, a few months later: the women in the church, rows and rows of nurses in uniform.

I dread staying in the classroom after my classmates go home; I dread getting in the car with my teacher – a violation of some sacred boundary. Teacher and student. It feels wrong to be this familiar with her, to get into her brown Buick, smell her stale cigarette smoke. I look out the window as she drives past Abraham Lincoln Park, past Holy Angels Church, past the old library, past Phillips Zoo, past the American Legion headquarters, past the Healy Chapel Funeral Home. The bridge over the Fox River. We are over there, over the river, another few miles and we reach the hospital.

This hospital was built in 1888. A Queen Anne revival with twenty-five beds. Three decades later, after the Depression, a utility tycoon, politician and resident of Aurora named Ira Clifton Copley donated two million to its expansion. By the 1970s it was expanding still, each addition in a different architectural style, side by side, awkward markings of time.

We take the elevator to the second floor. My teacher carries a peace lily.

The room has a window facing west, flooded with afternoon light. There is a table full of flowers, plants, Get Well Soons everywhere. My mother is sitting up with difficulty. A nurse places a gentle hand on her back. My mother wears a scarf wrapped around her head. She was bald, I think, she would sometimes wear a wig but now just a scarf. She was no longer beautiful, or not in the way I remembered or needed her to be. The nurse held the straw to her mouth, a styrofoam cup of ice water. I stayed near the door, watched her struggle to sip. There was a moment, seconds really, before she saw me, and that was when I saw her despair. The despair of the woman in that bed, my mother in great pain, knowing that she was dying, was imprinted on me for life.

When she saw me there, she forced a smile, said my name. Everyone left the room, the nurse and my teacher, left me alone to climb into the hospital bed with her, to cry in her arms. With effort she tried to turn back into my mom, to move beyond her suffering, to be there for me. But it was too late: I'd seen her face. I knew she wasn't that person anymore. She was leaving, her body in pain, immense pain that made no sense to me in those days, her body, my origin, was failing and taking her away from me. The mystery of her deep love for me and her simultaneous disappearance shaped my girlhood more than anything else. The early knowledge of love and death as inextricably linked.

A week later was Easter. My dad took us to church and then again to the hospital to visit my mom. When we arrived, the nurses greeted us, told us how pretty we looked in our dresses and bonnets. My dad went in first, and we stood in the doorway. Again, that pain. The horror in her eyes. Something I wasn't supposed to see. My dad hugged her, leaning down, and when he did, she grabbed him, held him and begged, a desperate, rage-filled hiss: *Get me out of this place.*

Witnessing my mother's need that day, her desperation, I surely recognized my own. Her fear was mine. I knew the depths of it, that it would never be fulfilled. I was eight years old, and I was learning that there is no end to need, no cure and no comfort. *Get me out of this place*.

(*Something About How to Be a Woman*)

Some weeks later. I've just turned nine years old. I'm sitting on my mother's bed. It is as if she has been told that it will be important, to teach me this before she dies. A laundry basket on the floor. Something about how to be a woman. She lifts two socks into her hand. Show me, I say. She can hardly speak, she is so tired. I hate her for giving up. You hold it this way. Fingers at the top, two socks next to each other. I'm ashamed she's my mother, this woman who can barely live. You hold them here, at the cuff, and then you put your thumbs inside. Like this, she says. She holds the cuffs, tries to put her fingers inside. I watch her hands, white and limp. She tries to pull the cuffs over and down, the legs through to the toes, or halfway. I hold my father's black dress socks. I watch carefully. I watch her try: you have to keep the fingers on one hand with pressure against the sock and you have to use your thumbs to fold the top of the socks back over the fingers. You have to do that, that pressure at that moment, two hands ten fingers working together, you have to do that in order to make the socks into a ball. That pressure at that moment. She can't do it, it's a failure, the whole thing. There's another way, she whispers. She folds one into the other, side by side, but this is not a ball that will remain intact. I do not want to know how to do this, that is obvious. This is not a kind of trick. She lies back now, closes her eyes, it is all too much.

(*How to Be*)

The philosopher Ian Hacking once described the shifting classification of the mentally ill as a 'moving target'. A disease is recognized and named. A doctor or doctors come up with ways to treat the disease. More patients arrive with the symptoms of the named illness. More patients and more symptoms. Soon enough, there's a cause linked to the illness.

Take, for example, hysteria: the first disease attributed to women, and first defined by Hippocrates in the fifth century BC. Hysteria was caused, or so the theory went, by the movement of the uterus throughout the body. The word means 'wandering uterus'. As a modern physical ailment, hysteria was redefined and medicalized in the 1870s by a French doctor named Jean-Martin Charcot. Charcot identified symptoms of the disease, naming and defining and classifying it.

The 'wastebasket' diagnosis of hysteria remained in the American Psychiatric Association's *Diagnostic and Statistical Manual of Mental Disorders* until 1980. The removal was a result of feminist activism and the emerging critical perspective on women's health care. (In 1973, the diagnosis of 'homosexual' was removed from the *DSM* and replaced by 'sexual orientation disturbance'. It wasn't until 2013 that sexual orientation as a pathology was completely removed from the *DSM*, the result of years of pressure from LGBTQ activists.)

Ian Hacking is specifically interested in the epidemic of multiple personality disorder, or MPD as it was called when I lived in the hospital. Charcot was instrumental in naming and identifying the disease in the 1880s, but it wasn't until the 1970s in the United States that the disease was recognized and treated by the medical establishment. Around that sametime, MPD entered the public imagination. Most powerful among the representations was *Sybil*, the novel and subsequent television film. A 'true story' (as the cover of the internationally bestselling book boasted) based on a psychiatric patient named Shirley Mason. *Sybil* helped create the diagnosis of MPD.

In 2011, a book about Mason, her doctor and the author of the novel revealed that the diagnosis, and the accounts of early childhood abuse Mason had reported, were false. Mason had acted out the personalities as a way of giving her doctor what she wanted. She made up stories of her mother having abused and tortured her. For decades the disease was linked to childhood abuse. More and more doctors looked for this cause in presenting patients.

Of course, Mason had been an unstable, troubled young woman. At the same time, Dr Cornelia Wilbur, the doctor to whom she was entrusted and upon whom she became dependent, was eager to diagnose and cure this sensational case of multiple personality disorder. Dr Wilbur teamed up with Flora Rheta Schreiber who would publish the book. Before the book's publication, Mason wrote to Dr Wilbur, admitting that she didn't have multiple personalities. The doctor ignored this.

The cause of the illness mattered to the narrative structure. In the book, as in life, it was only after the doctor coaxed Mason into remembering her torture that she was cured. After revealing the secret of her mother's abuse, she was able to integrate her sixteen personalities and live a happy life. Therapists like Wilbur found ways to define and explain the disease. By the 1970s, the presiding theory or explanation was that MPD was caused by an early trauma, most commonly physical or sexual abuse.

After the publication of *Sybil* there was an exponential increase in cases of MPD, which continued throughout the 1970s, 80s and well into the 1990s. It was only in 1994, and rather abruptly, that the disease was eliminated from the *DSM*. The diagnosis had become controversial, with many patients and families reporting that doctors had coached them into revealing 'alters'. While the disease is said to have been 'renamed', it seems more accurate to say that the bizarre specificity of MPD was absorbed into the more comprehensive diagnosis of dissociative identity disorder. After a decade of explosively high numbers of reported cases, the MPD diagnosis quietly returned to its status as a rare and highly unusual syndrome.

Here was Hacking's moving target: a patient is suffering, seeks medical help, the symptoms of that suffering are named, noted and treated, if not cured. (There was usually no expectation of a cure for MPD, as with many personality disorders.) The disease is represented in popular culture; more patients (mostly women in the case of MPD) present with these symptoms. Soon patients present with other symptoms, the disease is then reclassified to include more and more symptoms. The parameters of the illness itself adjust and expand.

When I was in the hospital, the belief in 'recovered memories' was at its peak. By the early 1990s, increasing numbers of patients recovered memories of childhood sexual abuse. Doctors encouraged patients to find such memories. I know that many of the women I lived with had been sexually abused, tortured or raped. I know that many had not been. I don't know who was telling the truth, who was lying, who was creating memory through imagination and expectation. I'm sure we all did some of this.

Whether or not these things happened, it doesn't take away from the authenticity of suffering. That was real, even if performed, or especially when performed. As Leslie Jamison put it: *Pain that gets performed is still pain*. It was our way of being in the world. It was a way to please the doctor, and, by extension, to receive care. It was clear enough that if the diagnosis of MPD hadn't existed, many women in the hospital wouldn't behave as they did, and wouldn't have those symptoms; but that doesn't mean they wouldn't have other symptoms, other behaviors, other reasons to be there.

I did not 'have' MPD, but I do vividly recall meetings with doctors who suggested that I try to remember what I had forgotten or repressed or blocked out of my childhood. What else happened? I was asked repeatedly. Take your time, I was told, day after day. Did someone hurt you? I was asked. What about your brothers? Your father? I recall a young resident in particular pushing me to remember something about the men in my family, something that happened after my mom died. I said no. I was shy, I could not make eye contact. She was gentle, kind. Take your time. I knew if I said yes, she would be pleased. I could give her what she wanted. If I had been traumatized by my mother's death, by the subsequent chaos and neglect of the years that followed, it was not enough. Of course, I knew that I had not been abused, not by my father or my brothers. It scares me now to imagine what would have happened had I said yes, had I created a fantasy trauma to please the doctors. They were, after all, so seductive, and I was so young and susceptible, with complete and naive trust in the authority of the medical establishment, wanting to please them, to give them what they wanted. To say yes would have been another way to perform, to be a person. It was clear, if I said yes, if I recovered a memory or two, it would explain everything: my attempts to die, my rage and my self-destruction. If I could make this admission – *Tell us your secrets* was the motto of the treatment plan. *You are only as sick as your secrets!* – then they could heal me, treat me. A kind of reward.

In the 1890s, Jean-Martin Charcot held open visits to the Salpêtrière Asylum in Paris. Doctors and health professionals, mostly men, came from all over to attend. In these public sessions or performances, Charcot would hypnotize his patients in order to produce their symptoms, tics, fits and vocal outbursts. Some women became highly sexual, touching themselves or gyrating. The women on display were mostly poor, disenfranchised. They came to the Salpêtrière for care, and there they learned to perform in order to receive that care. Some of his most famous patients performed over and over again. As Charcot's treatment and methods became popular and celebrated, more women in France were diagnosed as hysteric.

That Charcot's most famous patient was later revealed to be a 'fraud' (as in the *Sybil* case) seems beside the point. She was, rather, performing in a way that would get her care and attention. She was learning how to be in a historically specific time and place.

It would also miss the point for me to call my friend Jennifer a fraud. Jennifer was there when I arrived and still there when I left. She spent seven years institutionalized (and the rest of her life in halfway houses or supportive housing, which is where she was when her roommate started a fire, and pushed her into the flames). She was diagnosed with MPD, and we often witnessed her moving in and out of character. Some of her alters were more entertaining than others. (Jessa Crispin noted somewhere that for patients with MPD, one alter was always a slut. This says at least as much about what it is to be a woman as it does about pathology or madness – what Chris Kraus might call the dilemma of being female.)

It would miss the point, too, to call myself a fraud for cutting myself after I saw other girls doing it, first in college, and then in hospital, and after I saw how the girls in hospital could do it, how intense and extreme it was, how it entered my imagination – they could find a device anywhere, a loose screw or a broken bit of plastic, how then I would imagine new ways to do it, to compete, how we fed on each other that way, how we learned to be patients. I could scream or go mute, I could rage or disappear. There were things we could do and we learned how to do these things and the context made it meaningful. Is this performance theory? Is this why so many people in Germany killed themselves after reading Goethe's *The Sorrows of Young Werther* in 1774? Or why so many people in Sweden filed for divorce after *Scenes from a Marriage* appeared on television in the 1970s? Or why I and so many girls I knew started binging and purging after reading a Judy Blume novel or watching an after-school special or reading *Cosmopolitan*?

I don't want to say (or at least I don't think I want to say) that I was not sick. But I want to say that nothing is isolated, especially not what we call pathology; that we exist in context, of the moment and of each other, that we are fragile and fluid. We learn how to be. ■

Rae Armantrout

Debt Economy

1

Say 'The continuity and connectivity of space
owes its existence
to quantum-mechanical entanglement.'

It follows that existence is a debt.

Yet entanglement depends on the record
of a previous transaction
being accessed

which grows increasingly difficult
as the noise level rises

and scenes begin to merge
such that a daughter

is a mother
disappearing beyond

the cosmic horizon.

2

To put it more simply,
you've forgotten

what you want
to say

and the people
you wanted to speak to

are gone,
their images

an overlay

of grieving
and grievance.

I've been a journalist for about fifteen years, and I've spent a lot of that time writing and thinking about displacement. I have listened to people describe how they were forced from their homes by war and observed them trying to make new homes. I have reported on communities whose sense of home was being undermined by the ebb and flow of capital. I have written about people who have tried to assert belonging through nationalism, and about people who were the target of nationalist violence. I have also written about the way these sorts of events are remembered – or forgotten – in official memorials and in everyday life.

The longer I've done this work, the more I've felt that there are things I'm failing to capture. Are there ways to express what has been squeezed out of conventional narrative? The pieces below come from notes I've kept while reporting in the UK, Europe and the former Soviet Union. They come from interviews and from journeys, including to places members of my own family were forced to flee. Some notes were taken at the time, while others were written later as memories came back to me. I've deliberately mixed up the elements, so that images and voices from one place blend into others. ∎

Sentences like walkways that stop in mid-air.

Gold lettering to thank you for your contribution to the war effort.

A house looks like a home until you see straight through it.

We met at the entrance and couldn't decide which way to go, but it didn't matter because the paths formed a triangle and would lead us to the same point. It was easy to find our way through the building, since it was a standard design that existed in many different places. You could have walked it blindfolded if you'd been there – elsewhere – before. We walked on through, passing doors thrown open in invitation, and out the other side. There, we saw plots of rough land guarded by hoardings. Pictures on the hoardings told us that what was being built there would be unique but exactly the same. We walked on to reach a grassy bank, and suddenly the land felt familiar. Was it the way the breeze came off the river in this spot that reminded us of what was here before? A mountain of century-old dirt, possessions spread out for sale on blankets and sheets on a Saturday afternoon, homes built in the spaces the inhabitants had dug out from the waste. Would you believe there was once a canal here, carpeted in water lilies? I asked you if this was the spot and you said no, they dug it all up and reshaped the soil, it can't be.

She went back and they laughed because she spoke a language out of dusty old books.

She went back and the market was selling fruit and veg and meat, it was an ordinary day, you'd never have known.

She went back and it had moved, there had been a flood and nobody was sure where exactly it was any more.

Anyway, they had bigger things to worry about, the flood had caused a lot of damage.

She went back and they had built over the cemetery, they said they were going to move it somewhere else, were going to.

She went back and said nothing's changed, I thought it would be good to see them again, but nothing's changed, I shouldn't have come.

In the museum they told her story, but didn't mention her name. She tried to tell them it was hers and they said, Ours too, this is a concept around which we can unite.

At first, she said, I got caught up in the patriotism of it all. I saw it as a way of making a break with the past.

Our youth came to follow us, he said, and the paths they took told us they had given up on the world we imagined for them. We saw them escaping and to us it was like liquid running from broken skin.

They bring the country to the city, driving their animals with sticks along the lane. They put birds in cages and photos of fields on the wall to remind themselves of what came before. They leave their traces on faded tiling and painted signs that hang from first-floor windows. Others take their place and fill their rooms with light and heat.

The carved figures and the mosaics are still there, they've just been covered over with plaster.

We took jobs as taxi drivers, he said, in factories, as chefs, as teachers, in shops, to tide us over until the time came to go back. We waited to live, and we didn't realise until too late that the waiting itself was the living.

At first, she said, I was into taking selfies with soldiers. But then we started to find out.

You and I sat there and watched the mother and the baby stand in tableau behind the cake and the father hurry around and offer drinks and ask if we were enjoying ourselves. The father had waited three years for the mother, the mother had waited three years for the father. They put on music and asked us to dance.

He sent the story to me line by line:

My mother told me I should go.

They took us into the marshes at night.

We stood in swamp water up to our necks.

There was a rope to pull ourselves across.

I got a terrible kidney infection from the water.

It was fifteen years ago.

Arrive while it is still dark to get good seats on the train. Bring food for the journey. The fifth paragraph, your nationality. Everyone must have one.

The moving of the earth. In barrows. From one place to another.

*

A cushion of cloud presses damply down to smother the sky, to say we are nowhere and everywhere. She looks out of the misted window of the bus at the half-finished buildings and says, They're making this a desirable place to live.

Since the incident, she has:

asked for clothes 23 times

reported 7 deaths

expressed her disapproval of the police 13 times

posted 3 photographs of mothers and babies

invited 1,748 people to distribute food 49 times

accepted 237 friend requests

been tagged 57 times in order to draw her attention to something and 44 times in gratitude

posted 5 photographs of a short holiday by the sea

counted down the time to demonstrations, court hearings and funerals: in 2 weeks' time, in 1 week's time, tomorrow, today, here is what happened yesterday

He wanted to tell me faster than the words would allow. He was rescued but he left his phone behind in a plastic bag full of his belongings. It floated on the water for days, his parents were ringing him to find out where he was, the phone rang until the air ran out and the bag sank.

We sat in the cafe and he waved his hands and stubbed his cigarettes out in the ashtray one after another. The translator tried to help but she couldn't keep up.

We stopped walking just as he was telling me that he thought the media gave to war a logic and coherence that didn't really exist.

Oh, he said, I didn't know we would turn the corner and we would find ourselves here. It looks the same. But in my mind I can see the old woman with the megaphone – and the masked men.

After they'd sold off the furniture and rolled up the carpets and stripped the metal and the wood from the walls, rose bushes grew all over the abandoned homes. For a while, nobody came. Then the petals were taken from the roses and packed tightly into lorries; they were driven away to make perfume.

The notes belong to you, said the guards, but the paper you wrote them on is ours.

I took the motorway that ran along the ridge overlooking the bay. Pink and white oleander had burst from the verges and was hanging over the crash barriers at the side of the road. Tourist signs pointed the way to the ancient city, leading through a maze of empty industrial lots, then down a mud track. I got out of the car and checked the map on my phone, which told me I was in the right place, but all I could see was a field with a ticket office in one corner. Two elderly men were sitting in the shade of the ticket office doorway; they were surprised to have a visitor.

You can't see the ruins, one told me, the grass is too high. Someone was supposed to come and cut it but he didn't know when.

The map on my phone said: *place is possibly closed or doesn't exist.*

The screens in the metro carriage are playing looped footage of a territory they say belongs to you. The camera swoops over a wooded hillside and towards the shore. This place, the screens say, it is inside us. They mean to say that the place is within our territory, but everyone on the metro carriage knows that this is not the case. If it was, they would not need to play looped footage of it on the screens, swooping over the wooded hillside and towards the shore.

Above ground, on the concourse of the station, another screen is playing looped footage. It is playing looped footage of tank wheels running their tracks over rough ground, of a woman opening a door in civilian dress and the same woman walking into a room in nurse's uniform. She reaches out and touches a soldier lying in a hospital bed. The screen is shaped like a cylinder: four times around its circumference the woman smiles, opens the door and brings new life to the injured man.

Out in the city it is the first truly warm day of the year, and we walk through a long, narrow park filled with blossoming trees. Large, egg-shaped sculptures are placed in rows along the park, creating an avenue. The eggs are painted with designs that are copied from folklore, from wedding dresses, from infant smocks in old family portraits. In the park, parents take photos of their own children beside the sculptures and beneath the blossoming trees.

We leave the park and walk along grand boulevards that have recently been renamed. The names have been chosen in such a way that they are at once new and very old. These names have not yet settled: a stranger stops us to ask for directions and you become confused, using names for the streets that no longer exist and, moreover, are never supposed to have existed.

At the end of one boulevard we see a slope that rises above the city. You remember a story someone told you about a terrible thing that once happened high up there, right in front of the city but out of its sight.

When people heard about what happened their first instinct was to bury the evidence. Now, they build a bigger monument each year and repeat the story they have always told themselves: nothing like that could happen in a place that belongs to us.

As the sun starts to go down, people line up on street corners. They are waiting quietly for small vehicles that will take them to tall buildings on the edges of the city. The older people are holding saplings, some of which will eventually bear fruit, but whose thin branches do not yet even hold leaves. The roots of the saplings are covered in plastic bags. The bags are wrapped around and around the roots, keeping the soil that clings to them from view. ∎

BAGHDADLAND

Aline Deschamps

Introduction by Rattawut Lapcharoensap

I n the early 1990s, I attended a secondary school in south-east
Bangkok that was surrounded by large tracts of what used to be
rice fields. Over the course of a single school year, the country's largest
shopping mall at the time – Seacon Square – emerged out of the
mud-plain outside of our windows like some leviathan rising out of
a bog. Needless to say, my classmates and I were driven to distraction
by its emergence; my memory of the year is of a constant squall of
window-rattling construction noise, and the defeated expressions on
the faces of our teachers, who had already been struggling to make
themselves heard over the high pubescent derangements of sixty
ornery teenagers. (Personal PA systems would quickly become de
rigeur in the classroom, which tended to make our teachers look like
extremely sad buskers.) But we were also distracted by our equally
seismic ideas about what the coming mall might contain, especially
once its posts and beams began to give us a sense of its enormity.
Speculating about what that gargantuan steel-and-concrete skeleton
might house – well, it was far more interesting than anything those
teachers were trying to make us learn.

I thought about that year as I considered Aline Deschamps's photoessay of contemporary Iraqi theme parks. While theme parks are often understood as kitschy capitalist fantasias, Deschamps's photographs present us instead with the mystery of a human dream. In many of the photographs, the grounds appear somewhat empty if not deserted. There are few decorative accents and the attractions are standard amusement-park fare: a swing carousel, rollercoasters, a Ferris wheel, bumper cars. Few people are on the rides and nobody seems to be queueing up for them. (Nobody seems to be operating them either; we are apparently in amusement parks without employees.) Many of the images have been captured at dusk, and it is unclear if these are the first visitors of the day or the last. They are mostly teenagers or young adults – some mugging for the camera, others caught in moments of apparent candor – all of them handsomely dressed in their finery. Given the twilit atmosphere and the vast spaces available to them, the subjects of Deschamps's photographs look like they have arrived either too early or too late to a party. They look like they might be trespassing. The photographs do not feel like a documentary record of kids in theme parks so much as a startling lyric glimpse of some inner vision that they all might be having of one. They're not going to Baghdadland. They're dreaming it up.

And then there is the oddness of 'Baghdadland' as a name, which might at first seem like a malapropism or satire, like something out of a George Saunders short story featuring, say, beleaguered Desert Storm LARPers. But such a tonal impression would rely upon received ideas of Baghdad outside of the city itself, of what Baghdad might mean to non-Baghdadis, and the tone of Deschamps's photographs is decidedly *not* comic and satiric, nor is it solemn and tragic. The mood here is one of wonder and joy, and strangely for photographs of amusement parks silence and stillness. Many of her subjects are having a great if mundane time. They are simply being amused at an amusement park – the boy in the tiger face-paint, the young women laughing in their bumper cars, the young men in matching leather jackets and gloriously coiffed hair – even as others strike more pensive, introspective postures, like the young woman in the first photograph pausing to consider something just outside of the frame while her companion leads her towards the park's attractions, or the young man lost in thought against the towering backdrop of a Ferris wheel.

By using one of the park's names to title her series, Deschamps suggests a living context, a scale with which to measure the everyday drama of what's visible in her photographs. The name gestures towards what's invisible. It lightly specifies what's not seen. Iraq's recent history suddenly haunts the frame as a potential source of drama and tension. Beyond the lurid, artificial backdrop of Baghdadland looms another backdrop entirely, out there in the coming dark: perhaps Baghdad itself. But only perhaps. There's no way to know for sure since the emphasis is not on the public and the geopolitical but the private and the everyday. As a result, Deschamps's photographs feel simultaneously haunted by history and outside of it, and they evoke – for me at least – that early chapter in Toni Morrison's *Beloved* when Sethe, Denver and Paul D go to a carnival, with all their wreckage seemingly behind them, only to have Beloved walk out of the water in the very next chapter with her own ideas about what's present and what's past.

The pursuit of pleasure and joy is never an idle one. It is never without its ghosts. And yet the ghosts don't make the pursuit any less urgent or real – they may even grant the pursuit its meaning in the first place. Deschamps's photographs honor the beauty and necessity of that pursuit. They provide us with glimpses of young Iraqi people seeking flight, velocity, sound and propulsion as self-contained pleasures, and they suggest that the seeming uselessness of such pleasures is never an argument against them. The photographs bear witness to their Baghdadland dreams, and they suggest – by virtue of our participation in them as viewers – that those dreams might also be ours. ■

HUNT SLONEM
Untitled (Pink Rabbit), 2018
© ARS, NY and DACS, London 2022

FATTY

Dizz Tate

S ummer had turned to September and so it was time for my mother to bring a new man home. I could hear him on the other side of the wall, but his breathing didn't give much away about his personality. On the other hand, I could hear my mother's whole soul by listening to her sleep. She had a spectacular snore. It evaded every obstruction, rumbling across our house and, I imagined, through the thin walls to the neighbours next door. Sometimes I thought the whole road could hear her, and I imagined myself as one of a long row of neighbours in a line of beds, all of us tense and silent, waiting for the beginnings of my mother's next note. She lived her whole life with the same fervour as that snore. Her bedside drawer was full of disposable leopard-print earplugs for her suitors, and condoms that she ordered in bulk from Amazon, an empty teabag nestled among them that she'd filled with lavender stolen from the neighbour's hedge and a few drops of vanilla essence. I checked the contents of this drawer throughout my childhood, fingering the sharp foil packets, squeezing the earplugs small and stretching them back out again. Love was in that drawer, and sex, and these are the only two things in the world that have ever interested me.

My father left when I was nine. He had another family kept tidily hidden an hour's drive up the motorway, and when the two women found out about each other, the other one forgave him and my mother did not. After this she told me very clearly that she was done with men in a serious way, but she knew herself well enough that she could not do without some male attention from time to time. 'Is that okay?' she asked me, the only time the question was ever posed. I didn't really understand but I nodded and said, 'Okey-dokey,' which was the way I agreed to serious matters at the time. She kept her promise. She found her niche with men on the brink of divorce and brought one home for about three months each year, usually just after summer, when sun and skin convinced them to stray. She liked big, sad men. She took care of them for this brief confused time in their lives and then, more often than not, sent them back to their wives in time for Christmas, both exhausted and refreshed by her kindness and her coldness. I didn't mind the men. They sat at the kitchen table and stared at me as I ate cereal, smiling to themselves and blinking a lot, like someone who couldn't believe their luck and had to keep checking they weren't dreaming.

Since I'd finished school, I'd been working in a cafe in town called The Tea Room. It was in the basement floor of a failing shopping centre that had been there for decades. A jazzier, shinier American-style mall had been built on the other side of town, with a cinema and a fancy burger place, the kind where they sealed the two buns with a toothpick to contain the overflowing contents, and an H&M. I never saw anyone I knew at work, which suited me.

One morning I was on the opening shift alone, and had to be in by eight. I pulled on my white work shirt from the back of the chair, and rolled up the sleeves to hide the ketchup stains at the cuffs. I found the tights where the ladders were highest up, with only a hidden, gaping hole across my left butt cheek. I stuffed my shirt into them, then pulled on my elasticated black skirt that held in my belly and just covered my crotch. I sprayed myself all over with Impulse deodorant, a scent I had decided was my signature. It was called Vanilla Musk. I probably associated it with my mother's sex drawer, though I did not make this connection at the time. I covered my skin and neck in a BB cream that I'd bought a few shades dark to try and make myself look tanned, striped some glittery bronzer across my bones, rubbed rose Vaseline into my cheeks and lips and then ran a mascara wand through my eyelashes until they came together in dramatic clumps. My hair was greasy, and I pulled it into an aggressive topknot that elevated my eyebrows into two quizzical arches. I glared at myself in my mirror. I blew myself a kiss. I turned to the side, sucked in my stomach and pushed out my bum, following the curves with my hands, undulating them like little fins.

I didn't know what I was doing but I figured it would be attractive to someone, this aquatic dance, this bare and bold admiration. I loved looking in the mirror. When I looked at myself it was like I couldn't think at the same time. I was all body in there, enclosed in the glass, like a girl in a peep show. I didn't even care if I was beautiful or not, it was a body to look at, and it was mine, and I could move it in so many interesting ways. It was a secret life I led in the mirror. I joined in with the other girls at the pub when we discussed our faults, girls much more beautiful than me complaining about jutting bones in their noses or thin lips, but I didn't really believe what I was saying or agreeing with. All I had to do was imagine the mirror girl, like a mistress I kept secret, average and willing, brimming with unfulfilled desire.

My shopping centre, and I thought of it as mine, was a ten-minute walk from my house, straight past the shuttered high street with the DIY store, the newsagent, the pharmacy, the launderette, the bakery, the pub. It was one of the first cold days, the light white and crisp, full of back-to-school possibility, the return of order after the summer chaos. I was eighteen. I felt thrilled by the lines September drew, even though nothing tangible was going to change in my life that year. I liked the feeling of expectancy anyway, all tucked up inside me.

I unlocked the centre doors with my set of keys, feeling grand and important, like I always did opening up, like one of those businessmen or minor celebrities cutting a ribbon with a huge pair of scissors. The centre was silent, the beige floor freshly waxed, a smell hanging in the air like chlorine. Only some of the panel lights had been switched on, the rest came on at eight. I walked past the dark bowling alley, the neon lights of the two arcade games still flashing. Sometimes I saw girls coming out of there because the owner was a creep who let anyone stay over for a lock-in, served pitchers of warm beer to thirteen-year-olds if they popped a button on their shirts when they leaned over to tie up their squeaky clown shoes. Someone was turning the lights on in the ancient greeting-card place, which had recently undertaken new management and started selling penis pasta and sashes that read things like BRIDAL SLUT alongside the teddy bears and fake flowers. I drifted past the clothing store that had shown the same stock for twenty years, shapeless V-necks and slacks with diamanté belts, and then the kiosk where the blonde woman sold chocolate-covered strawberries, expertly dipping half-mouldy fruit into a stout chocolate fountain, handing them over to horny-looking men who practically ran home, their berries squishing in the box. But no one else was around that early.

The pet shop was dark, too. It was right opposite the cafe so I knew its rituals, its timings, as well as ours. He never switched the lights on before ten. I took the opportunity to creep up close to the window. There sat the joy of the shopping centre, what I thought of as its secret heart. A white rabbit. Her hutch took up the whole of the window, by far the finest display in the centre. Stuck to the exterior glass were two posters showing a slimy-haired magician pulling a rabbit out of a top hat by the ears. The posters were faded, giving them the look of an old romantic film, and the pictured rabbit was small, fluffy and bright-eyed compared to the real rabbit behind the glass, who was larger with a glazed expression that made her seem as though she was always caught in the centre of a sigh. She did not look as though she would take kindly to being stuffed into a hat, or being pulled out of it by her long, silky ears. There were star stickers adhered to the glass too, and THE MARVELLOUS MAGICAL F. . . written across the window in cheap red print that looked like lipstick. Often I thought it looked like something the rabbit had written on the window herself, like a cheap joke after a one-night stand. I had never been into the store, though I watched the rabbit often, and appreciated the novelty of the pet shop man's commitment to her story, as an ageing celebrity past her prime. The rabbit had become imbued with this story for me: the way she shuffled through her sawdust, seeming to shrug, her bright red eyes aloof and seductive at once, her languid napping schedule, the way she nibbled at her lettuce, like a woman who'd been on a diet for fifty years. She wouldn't have looked out of place with a cigarette tucked beneath her two long teeth, her water bowl swapped for the fizzing yellow of champagne. '*Darling*, I'm simply exhausted,' I imagined her saying when she shuffled along sleepily to settle in one corner or another. She was somewhat famous in town. Kids with no hope of affording pets came to watch her for hours while their mothers blew on cups of tea at our tables, their eyes glued to phones, taking advantage of the free wifi. The children watched the rabbit with such hope in their eyes, but the pet shop man gave them nothing back for their devotion. There was a sign in the window in big black print demanding ONE CHILD AT A TIME, and if one brave kid dared go in to try and stroke her, I'd hear the pet shop man's voice, sudden and bellowing from the dark of the shop: 'No Buying, No Looking.' So the kids stayed outside. I knew he still saw them, because whenever a crowd gathered he'd stumble over to the hutch, his hunk of a shadow hovering, and shove the rabbit around like some food on his plate he didn't want to eat. He'd growl her name, the one he'd surely christened her with, *Fatty* or *Fucking Fatty*, when he cleaned up her neat pellets with a doggy bag, always loud enough for the kids and me to hear.

I'd only ever seen one brave girl protest his style of care, early in the summer. She had two tight braids and a voice high with a belief in justice when she called out: 'Can't you be a little more gentle with her?' There was such a sweetness in the choice of the word gentle. It made me feel nauseous. I moved into the cafe door to watch, pretending to wipe the glass. The pet shop man picked up Fatty in one heavy palm, lifted her to the height of the girl's head beyond the window, so the two were eye to eye, and then let the rabbit fall straight to the floor. She landed with a soft woomph back in the dust, her hair billowing around her like a ball gown. 'Fuck you!' the girl shouted out. But the kids all scattered, screaming with laughter, when the pet shop man bounded towards the door. It was the first time I'd ever seen him enter the shopping centre's unforgiving fluorescent light, and it was only for a second before he disappeared back into his dark store. He had a name, and I know it, but for the sake of the story I prefer to call him the pet shop man. I've remembered him in so many ways. I've made him beautiful, disgusting, old, young, but my favourite costume to dress him in is the skeleton that was hung from the ceiling in my science class in Year 9, the one Lucinda Bailey was dared to give a lap dance to and did. I always remember that dumb joke of a skeleton as Lucinda rode him in a performance that stunned the boys into silence. It's the most harmless form of a human I can summon, that loose skeleton, that stupid puppet of bones.

I set up the cafe that morning, following the same routine I always did, unstacking the chairs, wiping the tables, turning on the coffee machine and brushing the encrusted grinds free, changing the toilet roll and squeezing blue bleach in the toilet, clicking on the Spring Linen plug-in air fresheners. This all took about twenty minutes of my allotted set-up hour. The rest of the time I spent making myself an elaborate coffee that included hot chocolate powder, caramel syrup and a layer of marshmallows that formed a pink skin across the surface. Then I slowly and leisurely cleaned the front windows, climbing on the chairs to reach the corners, and I waited for the pet shop man to appear in the window to watch me.

He lived above the store. He must have had a back entrance to stop him ever having to walk through the centre. The store was pitch-black behind Fatty's hutch. I only knew he was there because I could see the delicate white cloud of his breath, widening and receding, like some mysterious jungle flower, on a small square of glass near the till, a peephole between the opening-times sign, the ONE CHILD AT A TIME poster, and some ancient notices for funfairs. I pretended not to notice the breath, appearing right on cue as it had every morning I'd worked that whole summer. I reached cutely on my tiptoes to prise at a dead spider caught in a corner of the window, my skirt rising to a dangerous height, and in a fit of carefree daredevilry, I turned round, bent to pick up the window cleaner, and mooned a whole cinematic shot of my bum, feeling the cold air of September gracing the free exposed butt cheek from the hole in my tights. It was only a brief second, but when I turned back, the breath-cloud was widening, and even with my hazy eyesight I imagined I could see his lips, so close they were practically kissing the dirty window. Then I readjusted my skirt, clambered down off the wobbly chair, and when I looked back the cloud was gone as though it had never been there. Fatty was asleep, her long ears caught in her paws. Everything was the same, except for me, who had escalated. I felt enhanced and thoughtless and happy, like the girl in the mirror.

Mishka came in then, the only other girl who worked in the cafe. She was five foot tall, with peroxide-blonde curls and blue eyes that seemed to bubble. She stormed through to the kitchen. I heard the thwack of her bag hitting the floor, the clattering of her keys on the chopping board, the sudden blast of pop music as she slammed the radio on. She came back, tying the strings of her apron, which she folded in half so it was about the size of a napkin. She pulled her hair into two top curls with a child's felt scrunchie, reached for a biro and stuck it in the formed bun. She was always doing effortless beautiful things like this.

'How can you work without music?' she said, her voice accusing in a way that made all my enhancement blur. She was pissy, so I knew her date must have been bad. She stabbed at the till with her candy-pink nails. 'You do not know how to live.'

'What was wrong with him?' I asked. Mishka was committed to dating apps. She loved complicated lingerie and believed absolutely in sex on the first date, marriage after six months and never getting divorced. 'If you know, you know,' was her favourite thing to say, while she flicked through men or told me what fault she had found in her different contenders – some issue she had discovered, always before the six-month deadline. He was too English, or had referred to his ex-girlfriend as crazy, or forgot his mother's birthday, or could not iron a shirt. She taught me a lot of absolutes she had about men. At the time, I ignored her, but I've come to believe she was right about all of them.

'He said his sister was making *a big deal* about her wedding,' she said. She said A Big Deal in a honky English accent that made me snort. She smiled then, and seemed to relax. She'd seemed to really like this one. He was a fireman, and she often called him 'a real man', like this was a rare find in a sea of dolls. She brandished a nail at me. 'Never trust a man who says weddings are stupid. Every girl deserves a wedding and the man should say only yes, yes, yes, yes, yes, yes!' She said the series of yeses in a way that was increasingly orgasmic. I looked over to the pet shop instinctively, but there was no breath on the glass, and I felt a twinge of pride, like I owned the pet shop man and all his desires. I imagined a wedding between us. Back then, I didn't think of him as the skeleton, but more as a formless thundercloud, a dark mass floating beside me down the aisle, breathing acknowledgements of my beauty into my ear.

'Who are you thinking about?' asked Mishka. I felt hot and stupid, but the phone rang and saved me. It was our boss. Mishka spoke to him in Polish, but he always said the same things to us. He'd had cameras installed that summer, and he called about twice an hour to yell at us for leaning against the walls or sitting down when there was no one in, or to tell Mishka she looked sexy when she came out of the toilet at the end of her shift ready for her dates. I'd never seen him, but I imagined him as a pepper-haired businessman in an illuminated office full of screens of my body in a variety of slow-motion films, bending over to wipe tables, cleaning the spout of the milk frother with a damp cloth. I tried to make my voice deeper on the phone when I answered, and said *Yes, sir*, when he told me to stop slouching. I couldn't make my fantasy travel any further because he seemed to be a male incarnation of my mother.

The day began then, and I had no more time to think. The Tea Room had three different rushes. We had the regulars in the morning. There was a man who came in for a slice of white toast and a cappuccino that he liked to be all froth. He always told me about the weather in detail, including the predicted time of sunrise and sunset. I remember that day it was cold and dry. 'My favourite time of year,' he said, though he said that every time the weather changed. I think he just liked to have something to say. Then Georgie came in mid-morning when we were quieter. He always had a bacon sandwich that he'd have with half a bottle of ketchup and a builder's tea straight after. He had epilepsy and he'd trained himself so that when he was about to fit he'd raise one hand up high so we knew to go and catch him under the arms before he fell. He read long books about war, and would talk your ear off about it if you didn't have a distraction prepared. Mishka hated him, because he went on and on about Poland during the Second World War, saying he wanted to teach her about her history. Still, she caught him more times than me, had a sense for it when I was busy at the coffee machine. As soon as his fit was over, she left him in the chair and told me to take him a plastic cup of water with a sugar cube dissolved in it. She never said anything to him. After Georgie, there were a few young mothers who came in throughout the afternoon, the children rising in age as the hours darkened: babies turning into toddlers turning into kids straight from school. That was when we were busiest. We had a food menu that consisted entirely of the Tesco Value microwave meals we got from beside the station. Mac and cheese, chilli con carne, spaghetti carbonara. Couple of slices of toast. A sheet of oven chips, always crisping up on a low heat. A saucepan of spitting baked beans. Fish fingers. Hummus. The kids seemed to enjoy it well enough. They kept coming back anyway, making a mess, their mothers stuffing them with bananas and yogurt in the time between when they ordered and the food arrived minutes later, as if fearful the children would implode in fury if not immediately fed. It was my favourite time of day when the single mums and nannies were in. There was a pleasant warmth in the shopping centre, especially in the autumnal air, a feeling of yellowness, a warm place in the quickening dark. Even Mishka cheered up. She made a few cups of chocolate milk and warmed them up in the microwave, then came out of the kitchen to count the money and chat to me about her new date that night, an estate agent who ran marathons on the weekends.

She was still at the till when I cleared one of the final plates, one of the few stragglers left before we shut at six, a brat who'd only eaten two chicken fingers and then laid a bogie-sticky napkin over the salad bowl beside it. In the kitchen, alone, I thought of the pet shop man again. I took a bite of cold chicken finger and plucked the napkin off the salad bowl, revealing it had not been touched. I stared at the bowl, then slowly balanced the plate on the bin, keeping the bowl in my hands. The salad looked like the most delicious thing I'd ever seen in my life. The lettuce was the colour of lime, the edges frilled in an icy and delicate white, practically erect with freshness. The single tomato we rationed out over a whole day, one slice per salad, was almost a perfect circle, the fleshy, seedy insides plump as two lungs. I almost expected it to begin breathing. Curls of purple red onion intertwined round each other like locked legs or fingers, and a sour black olive lay tucked in the corner, puckered as a nipple. I held the disregarded salad bowl in my two hands like an offering, my mind traversing images of monks and beggars, baptism and stray cats lapping at milk, and I felt so overwhelmed with stimulation, so psychically and suddenly alive, that I almost dropped the bowl, but I didn't, I clung to it like someone hanging on to life, and then I quickly sealed it with three wrap-arounds of cling film, and stuffed it into my backpack hanging on the back of the kitchen door.

We were running late, the last mother was still sat there at five past six, sipping the cold dregs of her tea while her son sat cross-legged across the way in front of Fatty, who was leisurely chewing her way down a carrot like it was a Cuban cigar. I understood the mother's reluctance to leave, this rare moment to watch her son enjoy life without needing her. A fragile peace was drawn over her face. She wasn't looking at her phone, she was just staring at the boy, who was only about five. The pet shop man wasn't there, as far as I could see, and again I felt a surge of pride in him, that somehow he was feeling the same way as me, letting this mother's love play out, understanding it. I imagined he was leaving the boy alone to enjoy his fantasy, probably of taking Fatty home, letting her fall asleep on his sweetly sloped stomach, how if he could only take her home he'd be good the rest of his days. I would've stayed watching them forever, but Mishka went and swooped the cup out of the woman's hand and said, 'We're closed now.' No one ever argued with Mishka. When it was my turn to kick people out, my voice wavering with apologies and bargains, the women didn't even pretend to gather up their bags, just looked at me until I left and Mishka came back, make-up perfected and apron discarded, and they fled at the sight of her before she could even speak. The mother nodded at Mishka and paid. I watched as she dragged her son off by the hand. He looked over his tiny shoulder at Fatty like a romantic lead leaving the love of his life.

Mishka's dress that night was dark green, strapless and short, shiny with sequins. Her hair was extra fluffy, her lips bubblegum pink. She had a faux-leather jacket, the material thick as flesh, around her shoulders. She wore black tights and tall, thin, neon-pink heels. The phone rang as soon as she came out of the kitchen. She picked it up, smiled, said something in Polish, then hung up before our boss could finish whatever line he'd had planned to seduce her with once and for all. 'C'mon, I've got a train to catch!' she said, linking my arm and pulling me out the cafe door, still tentacled to me as she forced the big old key in the hole, punched in the code to lower the shutter. She bent over, smacked a pink kiss on my cheek and tottered off towards the exit and the sparkly blue bar of the station beyond, sequins dropping in her wake like a trail of breadcrumbs. She stopped when she got to the door and turned back to me, screeching across the empty shopping centre: 'Hurry up and live!' Then she was gone. The lights clicked on the timer and half of the shopping centre's panels softened into darkness. Everywhere was quiet and shadowy except for Fatty's hutch, glowing brightly in the pet shop window like a low-lying UFO.

I walked over to it, crouched down like the little boy to meet her eyes through the glass, but she was asleep. I felt the salad bowl dig into the centre of my back, and I took a deep breath, pulled down on the straps of my backpack, and walked through the door.

The bell clinked gently.

I didn't look at the pet shop man.

The store smelled like wet dog. There were no other live animals in there, just packets of brown food and a hanging display of bright squeaky toys. The shelves were half empty and looked sad. The pet shop man didn't say anything, but I heard the solid thud of a phone being placed onto a flat surface. I felt his full gaze on my back, and I could smell the cloud of his breath, though it wasn't the salty, lemony scent I'd imagined.

'I brought something for her,' I said. My voice was strange. I was grateful he didn't say anything.

I stood behind the hutch, slowly removed my backpack and took out the bowl of salad. I struggled with the cling film, finally ripping into the tight plastic drum I'd formed with my teeth. The salad's beauty had not lasted in my bag. It was limp and looked like a cheap salad that would taste of nothing. I quickly dug my fingers into it, lifting out the lettuce and shredding it in a green rain above Fatty's angelically sleeping body, squeezing the tomato, pelting the olive towards her. My hands were sticky. I suddenly wanted to get the job done as quickly as possible. I wiped my hands on my T-shirt, manoeuvring the bowl between them, and it was then that I felt him behind me, the bulge in his crotch absurd as it pressed into my backside. I started to laugh, a little hysterically, the lump was so *hard* and he pressed it forward so confidently, like a cat presenting a headless bird as a gift. His arms looped around my stomach, and he began to sway gently. I mimicked his movement. I was happy I couldn't see him, and wondered how I could picture this dance, what soundtrack I could apply to it. But then he started to try to twist me around towards him, shoving and patting me on the ribs and hips like he pawed Fatty around in her hutch. As I felt myself lose, knowing I would be turned without resistance, I threw my arms forward, shoving him backwards with my bum, and picked Fatty up. He didn't seem to notice, and Fatty made no sound, though I felt her body shiver in surprise. When he spun me round harder, grunting now, to face him, I held Fatty up in front of my eyes, not wanting to look at him. It didn't cross my mind that he would close his eyes to avoid the reality of me too. He must have done, though, because he shoved his face into Fatty's with such force that she screamed. I hadn't even known rabbits could scream. It was a metallic noise, the sound of prey with nothing left to lose, and I saw teeth, claw and fur rise up in shock, like a girl possessed by a devil in a movie, and he screamed too, the pet shop man, and dropped the handles of my body, and in the chaos I scooped up my backpack and ran from the store, turning back only once to see this new creature I'd created, the rabbit-headed man dancing around in the dark.

I ran, keeping to the squares on the floor illuminated by the remaining panel lights. I heard no steps following me, but I ran until I was out in the last glittering autumn light, everything dappled and glorious. The pub on the corner was busy, and everyone seemed to have a full glass in their hand, golden and sloppy. The football was blaring. Someone must have just scored a goal, because there was a note of collective joy in the air, like everyone was about to break into the same song. There was a tall lad in a tight white T-shirt leaning against the pub wall, struggling to roll a cigarette, and as I flew by he slurred, 'Happy birthday, lovely.' I turned around, marched towards him and caught him by the shoulders. I positioned myself on my toes and launched upwards, my lips hitting his at such a perfect bullseye that they both seemed to split at once, and our tongues and teeth and saliva met in a small and somehow delicate implosion, and then his friends, it felt like there were dozens of them, hundreds, but it may have only been two or three, were all cheering and screaming and applauding, and the boy was holding tenderly on to my backpack like it was a part of me. When we stopped to breathe, I didn't wait for him to speak. I wiped my mouth and continued my walk home, leisurely, swinging my hips, unfurling my bun from its knot, taking deep breaths of the clean, cold air, feeling my life as a sexual being swiftly begin, as though someone had switched all the lights on inside me. For a moment, I was floodlit, awash with this exquisite, strange light, romantic as a swimming pool or a football field at night. I was blue and stunning and atmospheric. And then the moment turned into another. The lights flickered, dimmed, didn't fail, but became instantly ordinary, and I was the same real person, no less excited but no more special, lit only by the panel lights of this unlikely universe.

When I got home, my mother was at the kitchen table. Her breath left a small fog on her chilled glass. She always kept a wine glass in the fridge beside the milk and the brown sauce. She would not touch a warm glass. There was no man. I could always tell when there was one in the house. She watched me as I fetched another wine glass from the cupboard, took the bottle from the fridge and filled my glass even higher than hers, almost to the brim. She raised the two careful curves of her eyebrows but said nothing. I did not sit down. I walked past her and ascended the stairs. I stood for a second on the landing, and then turned left into her bedroom instead of going into my own. I opened her wardrobe to reveal the long mirror that was stuck on the inside of the door panel, a mirror I never looked in. I perched on the bed opposite it, sipping my wine. The mirror was so covered in dust that it made my reflection look furred. The room was dark, but the mirror caught the street light outside and caused the shadows in the room to harden, splitting my face and body into a variety of anatomical lines. I stared at this curious, newly formed creature. I watched as the dust shivered and settled upon her skin. ∎

Peter Gizzi

But the Heart in a Sense Is Far from Me
Floating Out There

Hold on to the afterlife of the beloved, it's the only thing
    that's yours

Hold on to whatever magic in the backyard where we bury
    our thoughts, things of the world

Things of the world like an afterlife of the world to bury
    our setting outness

It's right to extract bone from the afterlife, dust collecting shoes,
    relics of the afterlife

Cut a hole in the poem to play peekaboo with the afterlife

Rebuild my house out of sky, blur my memoria into song

Make my headdress the right size to salute the emptiness
    alive in the beloved

The humanness of the beloved, the beloved and the night sky

Shapes floating out there becoming the beloved, the abstract,
    the total

Joseph Stalin and German foreign minister Joachim von Ribbentrop shaking hands after the signing of the Molotov–Ribbentrop Pact, Moscow, USSR, 1939

FATEHA

Sana Valiulina

TRANSLATED BY POLLY GANNON

Tallinn 1973
Amsterdam 2022

At exactly ten minutes to eleven I slip out the front door and onto the landing, gently pulling the door behind me, leaving it open just a crack. At this hour, Papa usually listens to the BBC in the kitchen, where the jamming isn't so bad. The radio is on the windowsill and he sits in front of it, with his back turned to me. Papa is obsessed with world events. A few days ago there was a coup in Chile. He doesn't hear, or doesn't want to hear, how I sneak down the hall. He's not the nosy type. One time, without even turning around, he unexpectedly asked where I was going. When I said that I just wanted to see if Mama was coming, he nodded his head and immersed himself in the news of the world again. I'm ashamed to admit that I can't sit still until Mama comes home.

If it's cold, I throw a coat over my shoulders. Then I run downstairs, go out onto the street, and walk a little way till I get to my lookout post. Lomonosov Street is straight, and you can see way down it. From my post I can make out the crossing of Lomonosov and Pronksy streets. That's where Mama should appear if she's coming on the number 3 tram. The street is empty at this hour, especially during the dark months

SANA VALIULINA

of the year. I stare at the crossing, concentrating on Mama with all my might. Three times a week she teaches at an evening language school to earn some extra money. Her classes end at 9.15. And three times a week I sneak outside, leaving the door open just a crack. Because if I don't go to my lookout post and watch for her, she won't come back at all.

There she is in the distance, listing slightly to one side, carrying her heavy briefcase. Mama walks slowly: her working day started at nine in the morning. She teaches in a high school during the day. I leave my post when she passes the entrance to the government ministry building. Now nothing will happen to her, I know. Lomonosov Street will carry her to me, like the current of a river. But she'll get angry if she sees me outside, alone in the dark. I fly to the front door and into our apartment. Sometimes, I'm so excited, I tell Papa: Mama's coming! I rescued her again, but he doesn't need to know that. The main thing is that we have survived one more day, and it finishes like a circumference, where the beginning and end meet. And that creates the harmony of the world, as Heraclitus the Dark says.

In January of this year, I struck root. How did it feel? Like resting against something warm. Like a new organ coming to life inside my body. Like something lost in me had returned. Like someone was calling from the other side of a river. And the voice has a name. The name is: FATEHA.

The name surfaced from the bowels of the internet in the National Archives of Estonia in Tartu, where I found my mother's job application. At the end of the 1970s Mama applied for a job in the computing center. Evidently, she was required to submit a list of all her relatives on a questionnaire. I had high expectations of the KGB archives – merged with the National Archives – where I hoped to find information about my parents. During the Second World War, Mama had crossed into territory occupied by the Germans. As someone with a dubious past, she was registered with the KGB. They summoned her regularly. But, not long before Estonian independence, the KGB

188

purged its archives – covering its tracks – so I had to be satisfied with only a few insignificant applications and questionnaires.

Insignificant – until suddenly I saw the name Fateha Bedretdinova. Born 1904, died 12 October 1943 in the town of Kingisepp during the bombardment of the Leningrad Oblast. That was my grandmother's name, then. Mama always called her 'Mama', and I never thought to ask what her name was. Perhaps Mama did mention her name at some point, but it had escaped my memory. So, for me, she had remained 'Mama's Mama'. Right under Fateha was the name Tagir – my uncle, born in 1931. He was killed at the same time.

For some reason, after finding their names, their birthdates and the dates of their deaths written on the KGB questionnaire in my mother's clear handwriting, it is as though I am seeing them for the first time. They are standing on the other side of the river. Mama is there, too. She is very young, younger than she is in the photographs in the family archive. But it was Fateha who called to me. From the moment my grandfather disappeared, at the very beginning of the war, and she and her four children had fled from the shooting toward the West, Fateha was the head of the family. Indeed, as Mama tells it, my grandmother always ruled the roost, although, by Muslim tradition, the right of dominion was the prerogative of men.

Now, despite her stern character, Fateha smiled at me and called my name. She has known me a long time already; I'm the daughter of her daughter, of course – the daughter she gave birth to and raised for seventeen years. Mama and Tagir are silent, but Tagir waves his hand at me, and Mama watches me attentively. So that's who my daughter will be, she seems to be thinking, if I survive the conflagration of the world. The river's current is powerful, but it doesn't bring Mama to me, as Lomonosov Street once did. We stand on opposite shores, and only a decrepit immortal with an unkempt beard and a bedraggled tunic is permitted to cross. But, as Heraclitus says, immortals are mortal, and mortals are immortal.

*

One evening I am standing at my post, staring at the crossing of Lomonosov and Pronksy streets, but Mama doesn't appear. As always, I left home at exactly 10.10, and now it feels like I've been here for an eternity. I can't go home – how can I leave my post? – but I can't bear it anymore. I'm frightened, and the fear in my heart wants to escape, wants me to do something. Now it's turning into tears. I can't even lift my hand to wipe them away, and I swallow the salty dampness that rolls down my face.

My feet come to their senses first. They take me along Lomonosov Street, past the ministry, past the entrance to the little guardhouse in front of it, past the gray residential building built by German prisoners of war – who also built our block of flats – past the Estonian television centre with its glass hall. The current of the river seems to reverse its course, and in a single moment it takes me right to the sacred crossing. At the newspaper stand on the corner I run onto Pronksy Street and crash into a stranger. 'Little girl, has something happened?' the woman asks me in surprise. 'I'm looking for my mama!' I sob. She says something else, but I run further down Pronksy. But Pronksy is deserted. Mama isn't there, and will never be there again.

Somehow or other, I run back to Lomonosov and dash home. But I'm not me anymore; I'm some other little girl. She flies into the entryway and runs to the door of the apartment that she left open just a crack. But the door is closed. She begins to pound on it. It opens right away. Mama. Her face is tear-stained. 'Where on earth have you been? What? Looking for me?' Mama is terribly upset from worrying, and she scolds the little girl and, at the same time, Papa, for not looking after her.

Today she came home from work on the number 4 tram. While I was running down Lomonosov, she came home by way of Kreitswald Street, which runs into Lomonosov on the left side, almost in front of our building. And now I'm myself again, and I babble something incoherent. I can't admit that more than anything in the world, I'm afraid she'll all of a sudden disappear, like her mama disappeared. And that's why, three evenings a week, I sneak out to rescue her.

*

And at this very moment, Fateha is trying to save herself and her four children, two girls and two boys, from fire. For in the river of life, the machine of existence, all times are present. Or, rather, as the ancient Greeks thought, in the realm of existence there is no past or future: everything occurs 'now', in the present, simultaneously.

While Fateha and her children are fleeing westward from their hometown, which has become the firing line in the war, in another city on the Sea of Azov, hospitals and theaters – where thousands of people are hiding – are under bombardment. Unidentified bodies are buried in hastily dug trenches – committed to the earth before the next bombardment. Five volunteers, who have rescued abandoned animals, are forced to leave their shelter because of the constant shelling. They take twenty cats and dogs with them – leaving the others behind. Meanwhile, according to reconnaissance reports, a supersonic missile has been fired at a target in another part of the country for the first time.

Now I look at Fateha and her children. They are running through the world conflagration, unleashed by a devotee of marches with a frenzied gaze and a little toothbrush mustache. The fire has devoured the world, and the world is dying. Fateha and her children have reached German-occupied Kingisepp, a town west of Leningrad. They carry provisions in a baby carriage and on their backs.

In Kingisepp they settle in a house abandoned by its owners. Fateha, Mama and her sister work for the Germans. Mama speaks good German, which she learned in school. For, in fact, there were two lovers of marches. The one with the toothbrush mustache, and the other, with a mustache like a chevron, were bosom buddies, and swapped entire countries to seal their friendship. The boys are still too small to work. Mama washes the floors in the staff headquarters, which is always full of German officers. They fart with impunity. Who says it's improper? On the contrary – it's nature. And everything in the world takes place, and should take place, according to its laws: both natural functions and the destruction of weaker organisms and inferior races.

On 12 November 1943, Fateha and her sons stayed home, and Mama and her sister went to help clear the road to the forest. While they were at work, a Soviet bomber was shot down. To release some ballast, it dropped its bombs while flying above the house that Fateha and Tagir were in. The younger brother had just climbed a tree; the blast knocked him out of it, but he survived. Eternity is a playful child, arranging pieces on a checkerboard, says Heraclitus the Dark.

While Fateha is fleeing westward with her children, another woman is trying to save herself from the city on the shore of the Sea of Azov. Cluster bombs rain down on it. She also has four children. One of them is her own; another is her niece, whose mother, the sister of the fleeing woman, left the bomb shelter to fetch water and never returned. The third child belongs to her neighbors. The child's parents were killed. Someone found him amid the ruins of the neighboring house and brought him to safety in the basement. The woman rescued the fourth child when she fled the basement and was making her way through the destroyed city. She found him sitting next to the bodies of his dead parents. Now all of them are with Fateha and her children, and they run through the world conflagration, through the perishing world. The world is born in fire, and returns again to fire, says Heraclitus the Dark.

Mama's younger brother, ripped from the tree and deafened by the blast, regains consciousness and runs into the forest, where his sisters are working. He will be plagued for the rest of his life by outbursts of rage, and he will end his days as an alcoholic. The three of them dig through the ruins of the house under which their mother and brother are buried. At this point in the story, my voluble mama usually falls silent – a special silence that I dare not disturb.

They find the bodies and dig a hole. They bury them in the earth, and her mother and her brother disappear forever. Fateha's Allah disappears along with her; that very Allah of the 99 names – Allah the Merciful, the Guardian, the All-Seeing and the All-Hearing – who every day, through her lips, never tired of reminding the children that after hardship comes relief. But the children of the brave new world know full well that religion is the opium of the people; God doesn't exist, and death is only decay and dissolution. Only Lenin, before whose mummy 200 million souls bow down, and Stalin, idolized and deified, are immortal. The life of some is the death of others; the death of some is the life of others, says Heraclitus the Dark.

Cemeteries and graves always frightened Mama. After Papa's death, she never went to his grave alone – only in the company of my sister and me. At the cemetery, Mama saw all the dead at once, devoured by worms under the earth. It was unbearable for her to know that Papa was also decomposing in the ground. When we go to the cemetery, my intrepid mama, who would rush into a drunken brawl to break it up without a second thought, holds us close, looking at Papa's grave with anguish and trepidation. The children of the once new world live in constant existential fear, without realizing that they do. They transmit the fear to the next generation. 'Just wait till I die; then you'll see,' Mama says in vexation, when she is hurt or angry.

On the weekends, in the morning, I crawl into bed with her – Papa is an early riser – and we exchange tender words and hugs, tickling each other and dissolving in laughter. We wrestle, and the winner, pinning her opponent's shoulders down to the bed, asks: 'Life or death?' 'Life! Life!' the loser always yells, begging for mercy. Mama hugs me, and I clasp her hard until my arms go numb. And even then I don't relax my grip, trying to protect her from death and decay.

The woman with the four children hurries to the evacuation bus, which will take her away from the burning city on the Sea of Azov. On the way to the western border of the country, the evacuation bus behind them is shelled. In a settlement some distance away, civilians are executed, their hands bound behind their back. Their bodies will remain on the streets, just as they were when death overtook them. The woman with the four children makes it to the border of another country and begins a new life there.

Mama, her sister and her brother also reach another country – German-occupied Estonia. There, they lose each other at first. The Nazi authorities try to send Mama to Germany to work; but a good German guard on the train lets her jump off in the middle of the night, and she finds her way to a farm. She will be a nanny for the children of the farm, and learn another foreign language: Estonian. Her sister and brother are supposed to be shipped off to Nazi-occupied Norway to work; but some local Tatars, passing by the refugee camp, hear them speaking Tatar. They return in the evening and make a bargain with the camp guard, trading the children for a bottle of schnapps and a piece of lard.

Mama, her sister and her brother eventually find each other again, and begin a new life in Estonia. And seventy-eight years later, my grandmother Fateha returns to me in the KGB archive. I strike root, and I begin a new life, too. It's always the same with us: life and death, wakefulness and dream, youth and age. For this changes into that, and that changes back into this, as Heraclitus the Dark tells us. ■

HALF PRICE OFFER

A YEAR'S SUBSCRIPTION TO THE IDLER FOR £27

HALF SHOP PRICE

PLUS FREE BOOK WORTH £8.95

Go to idler.co.uk/join, select PRINT and use code **GRANTA22**
Or call 01442 820581

SLOW DOWN. HAVE FUN. LIVE WELL.

NAZAR FURYK
from *My Own Private Louisiana*

SIGNS OF AN APPROACHING WAR

Volodymyr Rafeyenko

TRANSLATED BY SASHA DUGDALE

It was a long chilly spring, a strange spring, and we walked every day by the lake. To the west of the lake was the dacha settlement where we were living. Friends we had made in 2014, when we fled from Donbas after it was occupied by Russian fighters, had given us permission to live in their dacha, and we ended up staying there. So for five or six years our home had been a fairly ridiculous, barely inhabitable summer house, constructed by different owners through the eras. And in early 2022, we were still there. It wasn't really set up for living in, and it was about an hour's drive from Kyiv (between Bucha and Borodyanka, if those names mean anything to you). But it was beautiful countryside, with forest to one side and on the other a deep blue lake, about three kilometres long.

I remember very distinctly the birds appearing this spring. It was as if they had fallen out of the sky and into our forest, all on a single day. There were so many; more than ever before. I had not noticed such variety until then. My wife is an amateur ornithologist, she can identify many species and knows the particular details of each, and she, especially, was taken by surprise, and would spend time identifying each new bird that flew past our dacha.

Out of curiosity, and because it had become her hobby, my wife joined a Facebook group called British Bird Lovers. This small but friendly group of English ornithologists put up pictures: robins – we call them *malinovka* – and others that slowly became familiar to us. We learned their names and studied their habits.

But the behaviour of these newcomers took us by surprise. One small and nameless bird flitted along the road, chasing a huge raven. The raven seemed impossibly large, it flew low over the tarmac, and the little bird, no bigger than my fist, swooped down and attacked it with cries. The raven fled in disgrace and we were sorry not to have identified its little pursuer. I remember, too, a large group of storks. Over a dozen of them, they took up such a space in the sky. They were not in any kind of formation or flock, but at the same time they were clearly together; not just gliding in the insane blueness of the sky, but travelling in an extraordinary, harmonious trajectory, a dance-flight. The sight of them made me want to weep.

Strangely enough, we never even considered that this was not an accident, that the universe was attempting over and over again to tell us something. We were ourselves migrating birds; in a sense, refugees, displaced persons, without a home or a home town.

The rain fell incessantly. The trees grew so abundantly that it was almost frightening to observe. It was exactly what we had seen in Donetsk eight years before. Why had we been blind to it then? Why hadn't we gathered up our possessions and moved to Kyiv? I don't know. In fact, this spring, I did have some inkling that all of this reminded me of something, but I suppressed it, I put it to the back of my mind. I told myself that I shouldn't be superstitious. That I had refugee syndrome. I told myself that the coming summer would be wonderful, and I should give thanks and stop thinking negative thoughts.

Only a person can be so carefree, so unaware. I even had some experience. After our first flight I began thinking about how an excess of natural life compensates for death that comes all too soon. Nature seems to know the future, because for the natural world everything is cyclical. But despite all this, I let the signs slip by me. We didn't evacuate in time, even though the birds tried to warn us.

On 24 February 2022 at 5 a.m. Russia began shelling Kyiv, Dnipro, Ivano-Frankivsk and Kharkiv. A few hours later we were encircled. The only road to safety, to Kyiv, was the site of fierce battles. We were trapped. We later found out that many people had fled to their dachas, thinking it would be quieter there. But it wasn't: day and night the artillery thundered. Explosions shook the house so thoroughly that the doors opened as if of their own accord whenever a shell landed. Shrapnel and shells were embedded in the gardens and on the roads. A village about three kilometres from ours was occupied by Russian soldiers and they committed brutal atrocities. A whole large family was shot because they refused to feed the occupiers. The Russians used the civilian population as a human shield, firing their guns from backyards and gardens.

After a few days we lost electricity. The internet went down, the shops shut and thousands of people were caught by surprise, they were simply not prepared. On the first days of war, in our tiny village of summer houses, there were ninety-nine adults and thirty-four children. A few pregnant women, some disabled people, and some elderly people. We needed heart medicine, insulin and so on, but there was no way of getting it. In the early days a line of cars tried to get past the Russian checkpoint, with white flags on their bonnets and roofs. Some were successful, some not. It was a lottery, no one could predict how an attempt would turn out. We buried a family of two adults and two small children in our cemetery – they were the unlucky ones.

There were places in the forest where you could sometimes catch a mobile signal and we would search them out to hastily try to call our families and friends. Dozens of people would meet in the woods, all hoping to find a signal, and then all talking at the same time. One person yelled, 'I'm alive, Mum!' Another pleaded to be rescued, unable to comprehend that it couldn't physically be done. And a third shouted, 'I love you, I love you.' The person at the other end of the line could no longer hear them, but we all had tears in our eyes.

I can't write about everything I saw or experienced. I can only say that when volunteers were able to rescue my wife and me, to bring us to safety, I spent half the journey out staring at Russian soldiers at their checkpoints, tanks wedged between buildings, rural homes that had been smashed to pieces by shells. The other half of the journey I spent thinking about 2014.

We lived back then in the centre of Donetsk, by a park, and we couldn't help but notice the number of slugs and snails – and mice. In an industrial city, with a million inhabitants, the mice ran fearlessly down the streets day and night. They crossed my path as I took my morning run or strolled with the family. The rain fell in sheets. The trees blossomed out of season, all at once. The lilac and the chestnut and the elder and even the apple trees, everything blooming so profusely at the end of April it was like an image from Shakespeare, as unbearably clear as the Apocalypse of John.

Every morning I took my run around the town ponds and the birds chased me along. The ravens and the jays and other tiny birds. They swooped down on my head, harassing me, screaming and crying like children. Then they would overtake me and sit on the path ahead of me, still screaming. It was as if they were trying to force me away, force me to leave this city that was destined to fall to barbarians.

Much later I explained all this to myself as the effects of life's compensatory mechanisms. Nature knew that soon there would be death in that place, and she was compensating as she knew how. Nature fountained forth with the same desperate energy that would course through the battles fought in these places six months later. And hundreds of people died. And it will never end. ∎

THE

WHITE

REVIEW

'Nothing less than
a cultural revolution'
Deborah Levy

Sandra Cisneros

Having Recently Escaped from the Maws of a Deathly Life, I Am Ready to Begin the Year Anew

For the New Year I will buy myself a chocolate eclair filled with custard. Eat it slowly, with an infinity of joy, without concern of woe and tight underwear.

Susan's mother was directed by her doctor to cut down on salami or risk death. 'But, doctor,' she said, 'is life worth living without salami?'

For my new year I will sit down in the sun and dunk in my coffee a little knob of bread hard as my elbow, and on it, without concern for cholesterol, I will spread delicious butter, the kind that reminds me of Mexico City's Café La Blanca on Calle Cinco de Mayo, or the clinking glasses of El Gran Café de la Parroquia in Veracruz.

I will snooze with my dogs till I radiate love, for they are life's true gurus. I will wake gently so as not to disturb the dreams that have alighted overnight on the branches of sleep, and before they flutter away on soundless wings, I will examine and admire each.

This season of my escape, I will push my foot down on the accelerator of my life, *vámonos vobiscum*, and hurry to sit under a tree with a book thicker than a dozen homemade *tamales*. Henceforth, I will read only for pleasure or transmogrification.

All toxic folk are to be excised from the remaining days of my life, the *chupacabras* and *chupacabronas*, who are a purgatory of pain.

I will allow myself the luxury to laugh daily and in liberal doses to overbalance the bitter compost called the news.

I will cease waiting for someone to do something about the war, the walls, the guns, the drugs, the stupidity of leaders, and ally myself with citizens who practice the art of tossing their shoes at heads of state.

There is much I know and much I do not know as a woman at fifty-six, but I am certain I know this. Life is not worth living without salami.

Sandra Cisneros

Figs

For Dr Bruno Ceolin

Some words
trip me
in my second tongue.

I say
pepino – cucumber
when I mean
pimienta – pepper.

Confuse
ginebra – gin,
when I mean
ginger – *jengibre.*

And when
the acupuncturist
tells me –
El hígado enamorado
quiere decir
el cuerpo está sano.
The liver in love
means the body is healthy –

I mistake
hígado – liver,
for fig – *higo.*

I prefer my translation.

All's right with the world
when figs are in love.

JEM SOUTHAM
from *The Rockfalls of Normandy*, 2005

FAULT LINES

Jane Delury

My mother is only seventy, but she has the bones of a ninety-year-old, the marrow like lace. Ever since she fell when my daughter and I visited last summer, she has walked with a cane: a silver-tipped walking stick that she ordered from an antique dealer in Paris. She texts my daughter and me photographs of herself from Los Angeles. Dressed in culottes and a cardigan, she leans on the cane in the gardens of the Getty, next to the armless hunk of Henry Moore's *Seated Woman*, in the parking lot of a bakery as she waits in line for a scone, on her deck above the Santa Monica Mountains. Every other day or so, she sends us these photographs, mostly taken by strangers. They cross the country to Pittsburgh and show up on my phone as I sit in Zoom meetings, and on my daughter's phone here or at her father's house. My daughter texts back an emoji of a smiling face, and I text back an emoji of a heart. My mother, who doesn't know how to use emojis, replies with a description of the Getty's latest exhibit – *amazing* – and the bakery – *fresh cranberry scones!* – and the view off her deck: *sky clear tonight.*

My ex-husband kept getting lost when he was eleven. He would ride his bike to the mountain trails behind his house and take a wrong turn, lose track of time and space and not know where he was. This was in Arizona, his home state touching mine. One afternoon he got so lost that he decided to spend the night in the forest. A helicopter found him. My in-laws used to tell this story to show their son's persistence, which scared them and which they also admired. They called it the summer of crazy biking. But I call it the summer of their separation. His father had moved out the previous spring, and the son lived alone with his mother in their bloated house at the foot of the mountain. 'Don't you think you were trying to get their attention by getting lost so often?' I asked my ex-husband once and he said no. He said that he barely noticed that his father was gone. 'Those trails go on forever.' Also, he added, it wasn't a separation. His father simply moved out for a while. Early in our relationship, when I wanted to understand my husband, I looked at these mountains on satellite. The trails he'd taken resembled partings in a scalp, all leading back to a starting point. If I wanted to boil it down, I'd say that I left him because he always called that the summer of crazy biking, even when I pressed.

Six months after I moved out, my daughter stopped eating. That was two years ago, when she was twelve. She threw food into the garden beds when she and I had dinner outside. I found some old evidence this morning: a candy bar wrapper under the butterfly bush. I held it in my hand and the wrinkled, spent plastic made me think about mummification and that made me think about bones. The older I get, the more I see how one thing always has to do with something else, and the harder it is to sort or to explain or to boil things down. I'm sure that if I looked up bones on the computer, I would find many beautiful and interesting facts about them. Such as how they start soft in the embryo, then harden in the baby, such as how our adult bones contain the lead and arsenic we ingested as children, or that skeletons hold together only with the rubber bands of tendons. But these days, when my brain starts to flow in this way, making connections, I throw up a dam. To return to what I just said about my ex-husband: I believe that I left him because he called that period of his childhood the summer of crazy biking, meaning I felt that every serious conversation we had never addressed its real subject. But I also left him because marriage gets boring, because he and I were different, because I had turned forty and my father died when he was only forty-three, because I didn't like living in the suburbs, because I was selfish, and because I wanted my own garden in the city, even though when I planted it, I believed I was doing so for both my daughter and me. I try not to lie, but I don't know what to do about the lies I tell myself that I believe.

My mother still lives in the house that I grew up in, although it's been remodeled so many times that it looks different. But the view of the Santa Monica Mountains is the same. Turkey vultures circle, and clouds wander the sky. If you walked down the street, along a concrete culvert, you would find a stretch of the San Gabriel River. In the late 1980s, I panned there for gold with my father, who was a water engineer. He told me about the prospectors who'd once camped along the banks. He told me about currents and spawning cycles. He didn't tell me about the mercury washed in by dredge mining, the dead steelhead trout, the DDT from the valley's fields. I didn't notice the gray tint to the water. I didn't feel each summer get warmer. I think I was perfectly happy, but then I know it wasn't that simple; already, I was following my mother into bathrooms, inspecting the toilet for splash. She was at her office most of the time. She came to my bedroom at dawn in her suit, smelling of treacly, eighties perfume. She kissed me goodbye as, down the hall, my father made me breakfast. He went to my softball games and bought my ballet shoes. He drew the cat whiskers on my face for Halloween. 'Good eyes,' he would say if I found a nugget of pyrite in the river.

When my daughter stopped eating, her father and I took her to a hospital for an assessment. We waited, not speaking, in a room with plaid furniture. Later, as our daughter sat between us in the doctor's office, she picked lint from her sweater, rolling the strands into balls between her thumb and index finger. The doctor said she should live at the hospital for a while 'until we get these urges under control'.

My husband said no. I said yes. I asked the doctor if we could be alone for a few minutes. The doctor beckoned for my daughter. 'Come on,' she said, 'I'll show you the unit.' When I was married, I liked to think of myself as the calm one, even though my ex-husband was the true calm one. But in that small office, neither of us was calm. We yelled at each other. His face shrunk as he leaned into me. He said that I was going for the easier option, because that's what I always did. She was our daughter and we should take care of her. 'We don't know how to,' I said. 'We'll figure it out,' he said. Then the doctor and my daughter came back into the room, and the doctor ended it all by saying, 'This is what she wants. Of course, we can't force you.' She spoke to us gently and firmly in a tone she might use with people in restraints. Her father and I went to collect our daughter's things from our two houses.

The day the Arcadia earthquake hit in 1987, I was with my mother at her office, doing my homework on the other side of her desk. My father had died the year before. My mother grabbed me and we got under the desk. The building across the street was mirrored, and in the reflection, I could see her office building sway. I thought, *We are going to die*. I felt more curiosity than horror, and I'm not sure why, since I knew what death looked like. When the building stopped shaking, my mother hugged me and said, 'We didn't need to worry. It's earthquake-proof.' My father had stayed alive on life support for four days. The doctors thought he might make it. Years later, my mother and I were sitting on the deck when I returned from college, and she said, 'At first I was afraid your father would die. Then I was afraid he'd live.' She was confessing to me, and I didn't press her for any more honesty. I understood. My father was his brain, his knowledge of rivers, his newspaper spread out on the kitchen table, the books on his nightstand. He barely noticed his body, treated it like a costume. He ate poorly and didn't exercise. Plaque accumulated in his bloodstream, stopped up a vessel in his brain.

*

After the first two weeks at the psychiatric hospital, my ex-husband and I took turns in family therapy with our daughter. Sometimes, the sessions were joint. We didn't look at each other. Our daughter tucked herself into her chair, rocking and twitching her leg. Eventually, she told us what she had been doing. At her father's house, which she called 'home', she hid her food under the mattress, and at my house, which she called 'Mom's', she threw it into the flower beds. This had been happening for months. When she and I sat outside together and I looked away to refill my glass of wine or to slap a mosquito, she took food from her plate and tossed it over her shoulder. Across the table from her those nights, I was distracted by newness. I was buzzing with wine. I was happy that I'd finally left my husband and happy with my house, happy with the future that I was making. After that session with the psychiatrist, I didn't go back to work. I drove to the house and went around back to the yard. I looked and looked as I used to look for gold in the San Gabriel River, using my good eyes. I found a piece of bread hardened to stone, a lamb chop, a radish that had sprouted. Black bacon. This morning, I showed my daughter the candy bar wrapper that I'd found under the butterfly bush, and she said, 'God, that was a crazy time,' as if it were all behind her now.

I didn't have a name for what my mother was doing. I only knew that she was doing it. I never tried to catch her in my parents' bathroom. There, I only sniffed the air and checked for splashes of vomit under the toilet lid. But I used to follow her at restaurants. We went out to dinner often because she worked so late and my father couldn't cook. I remember being nervous to walk on my own between the tables, so maybe this started when I was nine or ten. I waited a few minutes with my father and then I pursued my mother to try to trap her in the act. Once, when we were on vacation up the coast, I followed her into the bathroom of a beachside cafe. She was hunched over the garbage can. I don't know why she didn't use a toilet.

'Did you throw up?' I asked.

'No,' she said.

I never asked her again. This was not long before my father's stroke. On that trip, he and I went hiking while my mother worked. We stood on a cliff and he told me how this had once been a plain with rivers running through it to the ocean. He explained shifting plates. That's all I remember of the conversation. I lived ten years with him, but I don't know much about him, and I never will. I wish I could ask him why he let me follow my mother at restaurants. I wish I could ask him if he smelled that smell in their bathroom. But I think I know the answer. You can know what you don't know. By the time we took our daughter to the hospital, she had lost twelve pounds.

For the month that she stayed inpatient, it took my daughter two hours to finish a meal. My ex-husband and I chose her food off the hospital menu together, the only conversations we had at the time. Once a week, we ate with her in the cafeteria. The food was awful – shepherd's pie with a glassy sheen, bricks of chocolate cake that tasted like cardboard, globs of Thousand Island dressing on iceberg lettuce. If she didn't finish, she was prescribed supplement shakes in chocolate, strawberry or vanilla. Watching her glare at her plate, I thought that she had done to food what I had done to her father: she'd made it into the enemy.

When I planted the tulip bulbs behind my house, I poured half a cup of bonemeal into each hole first. I try to do everything right in my garden. Some of the plants came from my ex-husband's house. He called me during a rainstorm and said, 'If you want any of that stuff, you should take it. I'm pulling it all out tomorrow and laying down sod.' I drove to his house with a shovel, and I sliced up the cone flowers, the daisies, the butterfly bush. I put them in the back of my car, slipping in the mud, as my ex-husband watched from a window. My daughter drove up with a friend, and I stopped crying. I hammed it up. 'Your dad wanted me to have these,' I said. I lied as easily as my mother once lied to me.

*

My mother was beautiful in her suits and heels and gold jewelry. Her wrists seemed to be made of china. In her middle years, her wrists thickened. Her legs thickened. Her upper arms thickened. I would come home from college and see the difference. And I was reassured. I'd asked her once in that restaurant bathroom, and I had no intention of asking her again.

Last summer, she met my daughter and me at the airport, waving to us, almost hopping. Outside, the air was smoky and gray from forest fires. The roads I'd grown up on were as bleak as I remembered. On the boardwalk, people rollerbladed and scootered in bathing suits, above an ocean filled with hypodermic needles and sewage. That ocean will swallow the boardwalk one day, but everyone rolls on. Californians have always been stupid this way or naive this way or resilient this way. When I first moved to Pittsburgh, people would ask me how I could leave my home state. Because the weather. Because the mountains. Because the ocean. I doubt they'll say that as much in the future.

My daughter and I unpacked in my old bedroom and then joined my mother on the deck for dinner.

'Look at that beautiful sunset,' she said, filling my daughter's plate.

My daughter started to eat in the careful way she eats now. I wasn't feeling what I should feel: gratitude for what we'd escaped. Since the plane had touched down, a feeling of unease had churned into anger. I was angry at the fires, angry at the strip malls, angry at my mother.

'That sunset is made by smoke,' I said.

I was the same way the next day. I couldn't come out of my mood. My mother and daughter did a jigsaw puzzle, swam in the pool, looked through scrapbooks. A family hosted a barbecue in the hills and the sky deepened to pumpkin orange. My mother said to my daughter, 'They'll put it out eventually.' I said, 'And then someone will start another one.' I didn't like how I was acting, but my mother's optimism infuriated me. I felt again my ability to be cruel, as I'd been with my ex-husband when I left him. I told him that I didn't love him because that was the easiest way to make him lose hope and let me go. I sat on the couch and watched him cry, feeling the weight of my granite heart.

I couldn't sleep that night. I woke up early and went to the kitchen. My mother was getting ready for her morning walk, lacing up her shoes. I said, 'I'll come with you.' She knew I was apologizing. When I was a teenager and we used to fight, our fights had always ended in a change of subject. We went outside to a trail that cut down to the valley. My mother said the turkey vultures were confused by the smoke and no longer made circles in the sky, more like figure eights. My eyes stung and my throat was dry.

'Should we be walking in this?' I said.

My mother said she'd checked and the air quality was only six out of ten today.

'I'm so happy you two came,' she said. She was choosing her words and I thought, *She's afraid of me.* This only made me angrier.

'Of course,' I said.

'She seems to be doing well.'

'She is now,' I said. 'You know, it's a sneaky disease.'

I said *you know* in an offhand tone. I'd moved in front of her on the trail, my back straight and hard as a wall I wanted her to run into.

To create an earthquake, plates move for millennia. To create fires that won't stop, kindling builds up and temperatures rise every year. To trip and fall when you are seventy on a rocky path downhill is only a question of taking the wrong step.

I called 911. Then I called my daughter. On the trail, my mother was turned to the side, holding her hip and moaning. She couldn't make a sentence. 'You're all right, Mom,' I said. 'You're all right.' Her face was tight, closed, curled like a flower bud. 'I'm here,' I said. I didn't understand how she could be in so much pain. I thought she must have broken her hip. For no good reason, her face reminded me of my father's face in the hospital bed. I started to panic. And there, down the trail, my daughter was running, sprinting, her long hair flying, her long legs bouncing. I held my mother's hand as my daughter narrated what was happening. 'The ambulance is here, Grandma. It'll be OK.' I realized that this was how people must have talked to my daughter in the hospital. We are taking your weight now. The needle is about to go in. Watching her with my mother, I thought that I was starting to lose her again, but in the way that you are supposed to lose your children.

It is my fault that my daughter stopped eating after I left her father. It is his fault for always saying it was the summer of crazy biking. It is my mother's fault for saying she was simply going to the bathroom. It is her parents' fault for neglecting her when she was a child. It is my fault for leaving my husband. It is his fault for letting me leave. He said, 'Why,' and the next thing I knew, he was saying, 'Fine. Go.' It is the fault of brain chemistry, the fault of genes. And, I suppose, it's my father's fault too.

A nurse wheeled my mother to an examining room with a white curtain. I sat in a chair next to my daughter. The nurse parked my mother by the computer monitor. 'Can you describe the fall?' the doctor asked, and my mother said that she'd tripped and landed on her right side.

'And how is the pain, from one to ten?'

My mother said, 'Two now.' Her face had unclenched in the ambulance. She gave her age and answered more questions about the fall. The nurse took her for an X-ray.

'We want to get a good look at that hip,' the doctor said.

'Do you think it's broken?' my daughter asked when they'd gone.

'Maybe,' I said. 'If so, she might need surgery. If so, we should call your dad.'

'I already texted him,' my daughter said.

For a moment, I wished that I hadn't left.

'You'll have to go back for school,' I said. 'I'll stay here with Grandma, work remotely, fly to see you weekends, fly you out. Then we'll move her to Pittsburgh.'

'It'll be OK, Mom,' my daughter said. She knew I was already worrying about the idea of our being apart.

When he came back, the doctor said he'd seen no breaks or fractures. 'But I'd like you to have a scan. Your bones look weak.'

'I know,' my mother said. 'I'm on medication.'

The door closed again, and the three of us sat in the room. The X-ray glowed on the screen. My mother looked at my daughter. 'My bones are like that because I had an eating disorder. Not like yours. I made myself throw up. Then, like you, I got well.'

The nurse helped us out of the hospital and my daughter and I eased my mother into a taxi. We drove home, on the freeway, past the river. We walked my mother up the stairs, one tread, then the next.

'I feel like such a bother,' she said.

'You're not a bother. You're my mother,' I said, pronouncing it as if it rhymed.

I settled her on the couch with an ice pack. I went to my old bedroom. I took off my shoes and lay down on the bed. My daughter came in and sat next to me.

'Did you know?' she asked.

'Yes,' I said.

She took off her shoes, and I pulled back the covers. She crawled into the bed. Then, our bodies aligned and her head on my arm, we fell asleep together. ■

The art of seeing clearly

LOTTIE HAMPSON
Untitled, 2020

A WOLF IN THE FOREST WANTS

Sarah Moss

There are gaps in my memory.

I went to A & E that day because of the chest pain. I had tried to go running as usual, along the south Dublin coast road and up Killiney Hill, but it didn't work. My legs wouldn't run. My heart didn't pick up the pace. My lungs didn't fill. My chest hurt, more than it had hurt cycling up the hill to work the day before. I biked to the hospital anyway, because it didn't occur to me to think of an alternative form of transport.

I went to A & E because the book-stuffed hand luggage I could hardly lift turned out to weigh six kilos. Because my hair was falling out and my fingernails disintegrating, because my skin cracked and didn't heal. Because I kept losing my voice, though I kept going with teaching and literary festivals anyway.

It was morning, the brisk hour in which other people were arriving at school and work, shops and offices opening and I in Accident and Emergency, although I had not had an accident and felt no emergency. October: the day after my birthday, which we had not celebrated because I was too tired. Gentle rain, fallen leaves slippery on the road. I thought they would probably listen to my heart, tell me there was nothing wrong and send me home, where I would continue until there was something wrong.

After I had waited a couple of hours a nurse took a finger-prick test and then tried to give me dextrose tablets which I refused because of the calories. Orange juice then, she said, but you know how nasty hospital orange juice will be and anyway I don't drink calorie liquids. She took my pulse and frowned and took it again and then sent me back to the waiting room, where I pulled out of my bag the book I was reviewing for an English newspaper and went on reading, waves of condensation from my mask rising and falling on my glasses.

In the late afternoon someone came round the waiting room with a trolley of sandwiches, cups of tea, biscuits. No thank you, I said. Take something, he said, there'll be nothing more till morning. No thank you, I said.

L ater, dusk fallen and the street lights on outside, someone called my name. He led me through to Resuscitation, though I did not need to be resuscitated and was still expecting to sleep, eventually, in my own bed. They did the finger-prick test again and tried to give me dextrose tablets again, and this time when I refused they said they were going to put a cannula in my arm in case they needed quick access to my veins later. You won't, I said, I'm fine, and they had the kindness not to point out that if I was fine I had no business in A & E. I don't need a cannula, I said, and actually I think I might go home now, it's time I was cooking the dinner. They called another man, one who sat beside me and spoke kindly and directly where the others had been stiff, and I was for some reason shocked that they had sent me a psychiatric nurse. We'd rather you didn't go home, he said, in our experience someone in your state is on the edge of a precipice, people deteriorate very suddenly at about this point, your blood test shows us your organs are already failing, and if you're here we can look after you. You're not looking after me, I wanted to say, I just spent nine hours sitting in the waiting room, you can't say my state is critical when it suits you and trivial when it doesn't, but I said I'm fine, really, I feel fine, this was a silly mistake, I should just go home and get on with my life, I think if I go home now I'll be able to eat. Hmm, he said, and how's that been working for you, these last few months, and even there on the edge of my precipice I could just about see that he had a point.

Later, they had put me on a trolley in A & E and they had put the trolley in a cupboard. I didn't much mind. I'd flown back from a work trip two days earlier and taught my students all of the day before and I was a little tired. I should have been at home, cooking the dinner and keeping an eye on email and doing teaching prep in my head and getting ready to phone my parents and it was all right, instead, to be lying on a trolley in a cupboard, with three waffle blankets belonging to the hospital smelling reassuringly singed and two books I hadn't yet started though I was already beginning to worry about running out of reading.

Later, restlessness came. A man who was probably a healthcare assistant, junior anyway, saw me standing in the doorway of my cupboard. I need to go out, I said, I have to walk now. You can't leave the hospital, he said, which was news to me and not news I found in any way acceptable – I shall go, I wanted to say, where and when I please, I am in possession of the same rights as everyone else – but it was obvious that he wasn't responsible for policy. You can't leave, he said, but I can let you through the door into the atrium, see, and you can go up and down the stairs and around the corridors. OK, I said, sure, that'll do, and I slipped out into a glass-walled atrium with four flights of stairs curving up into a boat-beamed roof and as the door closed behind me I started running up the stairs but the running didn't work and the chest pain came again so I walked, fast, and found again, as I had trying to hurry across the airport two days earlier, that the muscles which used to lift and carry this sad sack of flesh and bone were simply not there, had disappeared, weren't around to do my bidding. I could climb the stairs but it was hard. My calves strained. I was slow. And my heart hurt. I went up and down a couple of times, around and around, proving points to no one, and then I wanted my cupboard again and after a few wrong turns I found my way back and lay down.

Later I began to feel odd, as if I were falling, the way someone might feel between jumping out of a plane and the parachute opening.

(If I ever find out if this is correct it will be because something has gone very, very wrong.) The fluorescent light in my cupboard seemed to dim. I was losing feeling in my hands and feet. I called but no one in the ward outside could hear me. It was becoming harder to move. I pushed myself up, hung on to the trolley and the walls and the door frame and after a while the man who'd let me out earlier saw me sagging there against the wall and came over. I don't feel well, I said, I'm dizzy. You need a rest, he said, and he helped me back to my trolley and pulled the blankets over me and then he turned out the light and closed the door. No, I thought, no, I need help, I need it now, but I couldn't speak and then there was dark.

When I woke up there was fuss going on, bleeping and a needle in my arm and a doctor doing something and a nurse asking me what year it was and where I was and what was my name. The only one I knew was my name, though to be fair I've been hazy on years since the first lockdown. There were several machines in the cupboard now, chattering and spewing paper, and someone had opened my top and put stickers and wires on my chest. What happened, I said. What do you mean, said the nurse. What happened to me, I said, and the doctor came over. Your blood sugar dropped, he said. You lost consciousness, about half an hour, and your heart rate fell dangerously low and we're running urgent tests to see how far your liver and kidneys are failing. Will you take the dextrose tablets now? I'll eat a biscuit, I said, it's a waste of calories, taking dextrose tablets. I was quite excited about the biscuit, which would be my first in some months. Whatever you can manage, he said, and the nurse said I'll get you some biscuits, straight away.

N o story starts in A & E. In the first place I had to lose some weight, though the reason for that was that I had gained some weight, the 'Covid stone'. It turns out that in lockdown my body went through the same changes as everyone else's despite running a hundred kilometres a week and working daily on core strength as well as all the stuff everyone does, work of various kinds and running the house and raising my kids, in which I include making from raw ingredients almost everything we eat, all the bread and baked goods and sometimes also the yogurt and pasta and jam and other things that many people consider to be raw ingredients. I cook with wholegrains, with organic ingredients, without meat or sugar, partly because I enjoy it, mostly, sort of, but also because that consistent daily work seems one blessedly straightforward way to be a good parent, partner and citizen, to use my resources to support sustainable food production and local small businesses, a form of caring for my family and habitat that's entirely practical and therefore can be achieved by habit and willpower regardless of mood and morals. I have more faith in action than intention. I like to be doing: writing, voluntary work, running, cooking, cleaning, knitting. I come of a northern English tradition that likes to be doing.

My weight had been stable for so many decades that at first I thought my jawline was softening and my waist disappearing because of middle age or incipient menopause or a more comprehensive core strength routine, and when I eventually thought to weigh myself after fifteen months of lockdown, which for me was also after emigrating and moving house twice and starting a new job and finding new schools and doctors and insurance and all of that, I was heavier than I'd ever been except in late pregnancy and I didn't like it.

I listened to many podcasts on science, including food and nutrition, and I knew the latest research on weight loss: basically, it's almost impossible and your best hope is not to get fat in the first place but if it's too late for that try some form of intermittent fasting. Allow yourself a window of eight hours or preferably six hours or even better four hours in every twenty-four for eating, or eat no more and preferably less than 500 calories on at least two days in every seven and if that doesn't work make it three days and if that doesn't work eat nothing at all on alternate days. Eschew ultra-processed foods entirely and refined carbohydrates and sugar as much as possible. Exercise because it's good for you, but exercise makes you hungry so it won't help you lose weight. I should try intermittent fasting, I thought, and since the eating window approach doesn't work if you run twenty kilometres before 8 a.m. and you eat dinner with your family at 8 p.m., I thought I'd try the fast days.

I'm good at fasting. I fasted most of the time between aged nine and leaving home at eighteen. There were psychiatrists then, too, though I don't know if the fasting eventually ended because of the psychiatrists or because of the leaving home. The psychiatrists told me not to go to Oxford, that the pressures of an elite institution would very likely tip me over the edge again but I was much more interested in going to Oxford than being safe, part of the whole cosmic bargain with the fasting and the studying had been that I should go to Oxford, and I was right because I didn't go over the edge and in fact felt at home there in a way that I never had before or perhaps since, though I see that feeling at home in an elite academic institution is entirely compatible with being over the edge and one interpretation is that I've been over the edge in some way all my life.

It was easy to fast two days a week, though it was hard to run on the fast days so I ran twenty kilometres five days a week and fasted the other two, at least for the first week after which it seemed easier just to fast every day, and as long as I ate before I ran – a piece of toast and an egg, usually – mostly I could get through the rest of the day on raw fruit and veg which wasn't really intermittent fasting but did the job, and on the odd day when travel or work meant I couldn't run I didn't eat at all so there was some fasting. I went on cooking for everyone else, more or less as usual except that I wasn't tasting what I cooked so it probably wasn't as good but there were no complaints. We spent a week hiking in Snowdonia. I insisted on taking my new digital bathroom scales. If I don't, I said, I won't be able to eat at all because that's the only way I can be sure I'm not gaining weight, at least if I have the scales I can see if I'm eating little enough. Yes, I do have a goal and of course I'll stop when I get there, don't make a fuss, and in the first of many betrayals I added, *women do this all the time.*

They believed me, I think, my husband and my sons. Why wouldn't they, when I'd been sensible enough for twenty-five years? None of us had ever needed to lose weight so they had neither done it nor seen it done. We thought ourselves exempt, in our thin privilege, in the bubble I'd cooked up for us in our obesogenic environment.

I weighed myself first thing and again before cooking dinner, eating only when the number was lower than it had been the previous day. Self-loathing roiled when the number didn't fall, adolescent rage that made me want to hurt the undisciplined body. I understood of course that weight varies through the day subject to hydration and excretion, but that knowledge didn't help. I needed lower numbers, couldn't believe that one small rise wasn't the beginning of a trend. I woke early to run up hills before spending the day climbing mountains at a pace set by sporty teenaged boys and the evening cooking for them. The Covid stone came off but I didn't feel safe at my old weight because hadn't that been the starting point, hadn't that body betrayed me with weight gain? Better, necessary, to have a safety margin, an extra couple of kilos in case of another failure.

Summer passed. We were vaccinated. Travel restrictions eased and I took my first travel writing commission for two years, flew to the Faroe Islands. I was working, including reviewing restaurants, and the goal, I thought, was to do the job properly and at least not gain weight while I did it. I got up in the Arctic summer dawn every morning, crept through the corridors of fine hotels in my running shoes and ran miles along the mountain roads, past sheep and clouds drifting along green hillsides and rivers falling into valleys, past Lego-coloured houses with white woodwork and turf roofs, past chickens still shut up for the night, past dark sea lapping a stony shore. I was happy running as I am often happy running, the rhythms of feet and heart and thought settling around each other, beats steadying on road and mind and body, and back at the hotels I showered in the magnificent showers and then went to breakfast, though in the second hotel I could no longer cope with being seen to eat and instead took a slice of the delicious dark rye bread you can't get outside the Nordic countries back to my room. I spent the days hiking, or on and off buses and ferries visiting the people I was writing about, the knitters and farmers and craftspeople of the islands. On the evenings when I was supposed to eat at restaurants, I did. I tasted everything and finished nothing, except one night when I'd run twenty kilometres and climbed three mountains and I managed to leave half of my bacalao fritters and my aubergine with pesto and my broccoli with romesco but I ate one slice of excellent sourdough bread with sweet Faroese butter and then another and then another until the basket was empty.

I came home. It was still the school holidays so I tried to combine coaxing the boys out of their rooms and off their computers with thinking about the book I was going to write next and, ideally, starting to write it. Neither of these endeavours was successful and it now occurs to me that both were hobbled by my prior commitment to losing weight. I took the boys on road trips around Ireland, getting up at dawn to run before eating fruit for breakfast while they piled through the full Irish. I made myself half sandwiches with shavings of low-fat cheese for our picnic lunches, and hoped the boys didn't notice that I was eating half my half sandwich, though I also hoped they didn't notice that I was eating chocolate at bedtime, reward for having made it through the day with an energy deficit but a reward that incurred the obligation to do the same again tomorrow.

I didn't write. I reread the books I'd read as research for a new novel. I made new notes that were very similar to the old ones. I planned my teaching for the coming term, wrote book reviews and essays, did what I'd said I would do when I'd said I would do it, as always, but I couldn't see the next novel.

The day I drove the boys back from Kerry, six hours right across the country, I didn't eat at all. I hadn't taken the scales on that trip, not wanting the boys to know that I needed to know my weight every day and preferably before every meal, that I now needed a number to give me permission to eat or tell me how much I could eat, and since we were sharing rooms I wouldn't be able to sneak the scales in and out of the car or hide them in a bathroom. Coming home, I feared the imminent reckoning, wanted to be as light as possible for the machine that had become my judge. I ran that morning, got up and crept out of the room with a clear three hours ahead of me because the route I had in mind, around the two lakes we'd been seeing from the mountains all week, was nearer thirty-five than twenty kilometres. I'd learnt by then that even – especially – on days when food was frightening, or days after food had been frightening, I could run as far and fast as usual if I tucked a toffee into my cheek as I set off, and while usually I wouldn't have eaten anything I like as much as I like toffee it was safe enough while running, no risk that one toffee would lead to another or to biscuits or breakfast, to the unleashing of my monstrous appetite. I unwrapped my toffee, took a moment to smell the wrapper, to anticipate the joy of its chewy, glottal texture and the sugar that would soon infuse every cell, the moment of relief and elation as my body would recognise fuel. (I used to make toffee with my grandmother, when I was a little girl and stayed with my grandparents in the school holidays. We used to make Dutch butter cake and lemon drizzle cake and what my mother and grandmother called 'fattening cake', which I would later recognise as millionaire's shortbread, and at Christmas we made mince pies and fruit cake; simnel cake with the baked marzipan at Easter and she'd make an extra couple of apostles just for me, because of how much I loved marzipan; Victoria sponge cakes with cream and fresh strawberries when my grandfather took us strawberry picking in summer; proper dark Yorkshire parkin, apple pies and our own toffee apples in the October half-term. If I was hungry between meals, or just if I asked for something to eat, my grandmother would spread butter and golden syrup on the white bread her milkman delivered twice weekly, two slices if I wanted them, no questions asked. We didn't eat snacks at home, or cake. There was certainly no white bread or butter or golden syrup. Some days we couldn't have lunch, because *there'll be a big dinner later* or because we'd eaten too much breakfast and *couldn't possibly need lunch after all that*.)

I set off, ran out along the main road to the turn for the track around the lake, passed hotels where people who didn't have to run a hundred kilometres a week slept their way towards bacon and eggs, smoked salmon and soda bread, towards Irish scones with butter and jam, towards waffles and syrup, porridge with honey and cream, the food of other and better people that I wanted in the way a wolf in the forest wants the meat you cook on your campfire. I found the trail through the woods and followed it, alert for dogs and dog walkers but also listening to my podcast which was, as usual, about obesity and nutrition. Fast. Control your blood sugar level, your appetite, your body. Make rules and keep them. Discipline yourself to resist your obesogenic environment. It's fine to exercise while fasting, good for you, teaches your body to burn fat. I shouldn't need my toffee, but I had learnt that without it I could simply fail on hills, be unable to wring from my blood the sugar to keep moving my legs. Better, surely, even the obesity experts would say, to eat a thirty-calorie sweet and burn 1,000 calories on a half-marathon than resist the sugar and have to walk after ten kilometres? What would Michael Mosley, now curled in my ear telling me not to eat breakfast, say?

My feet ran on and I settled into being alone in the woods, into the quiet of water and trees and sky. It was raining a little, enough to patter on the leaves and cool my skin, to pattern the lake.

Later, on the way back, trying to avoid running down the side of a fast road with no pavement, I got lost. Disdaining satnav, geolocation and being tracked by Apple and Google and whoever else buys access to my data, I do still get lost, especially running in new places, and I don't mind. It's good for you, to get lost, to be disoriented and to find yourself. I had time and I would have to have energy because there was no alternative. I ended up running part of the hiking trail through the hills and then what turned into a loop around the grounds of a stately home hours before it opened to the public, startling the gardeners and incurring the rage of the woman at the gate as I left. By the time I got back to the hotel I'd texted the boys to go ahead with breakfast, have whatever they wanted, I'd barely have time to shower and pack before checkout, and in my head the voice was saying serves you right, stupid and greedy, taking all this time to yourself, if you think you're hungry now you'll find out what hungry means by the end of the day.

We set off. I put my sweets in the pocket of the driver's door, so that if or more realistically when my energy levels fell to the point of being unable to drive I could have one, or half of one. Bad for your blood sugar and your teeth, leads to diabetes and obesity, but the sugar felt safe, straight to the bloodstream, no weight in the stomach, and I wasn't eating them recreationally, only when my physical capacity to do what was needed in that moment failed.

We put on music, chatted, enjoyed seeing our new country after the winter of lockdown. For seven months residents of Dublin had been forbidden to go more than five kilometres from home and here we were, out on the open road, gone west. We got stuck behind tractors and imagined the joy of driving your combine harvester along a narrow winding road while a queue of cars with Dublin plates weave and jostle behind you. I offered other drivers tips on better driving, caused uproarious delight by referring to someone who overtook us dangerously and flashed yellow rear number plates as he spun round the blind bend ahead as an *English wanker*. How do you know he's not from the North, Mum? What makes you so sure it's a man? Women can be wankers too. Can't. Can. Mum, can women be wankers?

By the time we approached the M50 things were less jolly. One child wanted a break and the other just wanted to get home. I was spacing out, forgetting what I was doing, not sure if I was driving competently on autopilot or in danger of passing out, but I didn't want a sweet, didn't want to give in to my body and its desires. I sped up, started overtaking so I had to concentrate, but I was cold and shaky. I knew this was utterly stupid. I knew I was endangering the two people I love most, and everyone else on the road, in the service of a pointless compulsion. I knew that if I really couldn't eat I should pull over and call someone, and that anyone with a shred of integrity or responsibility would simply ask the boys to pass her a sandwich or a cereal bar from the bag of food on which they had been snacking.

It was not simple. I kept driving. As we came off the motorway the traffic light at the roundabout changed and I stopped the car.

Mum, said my son, it's green, it just turned green. Sorry, I said, I'm tired, better that way round than the other, hey? But he was still looking at me, and I needed him to tell me the way home because I couldn't remember the roads.

Later, I told my friend about it. You know that's a safeguarding issue, she said, you know you crossed a red line there. I had the sweets, I said, I'd have eaten one if I really needed it. You needed a couple of cheese sandwiches and a chocolate bar, she said. You need help.

I need, I said, to lose some more weight. It took me a further three months to cycle to A & E. ■

CONTRIBUTORS

Rae Armantrout's most recent poetry collections are *Finalists, Conjure* and *Wobble*. In 2010 her book *Versed* won the Pulitzer Prize for Poetry and the National Book Critics Circle Award. She is the current judge of the Yale Younger Poets Prize.

Sandra Cisneros is a poet, writer, performer and artist. A new collection of her poetry, *Woman Without Shame*, is forthcoming from Knopf.

Aidan Cottrell-Boyce was born in Liverpool. He is the author of *Jewish Christians in Puritan England* and *Israelism in Modern Britain*. His short fiction has appeared in the *White Review*. He currently works as a postdoctoral research fellow at St Mary's University in London.

Jane Delury is the author of *The Balcony*, which won the 2019 Sue Kaufman Prize for First Fiction from the American Academy of Arts and Letters. Her next novel, *Hedge*, is forthcoming in 2023.

Aline Deschamps is a Thai-French photographer currently based in Beirut, Lebanon. She is a Canon Ambassador, and a member of Women Photograph, Middle East Images and Diversify Photo.

Thomas Duffield is a photographer and researcher from the north of England, currently based in London. His photography was shortlisted for the 2021 Wellcome Photography Prize and he was a 2019 winner of Portrait of Britain.

Sasha Dugdale is a poet and translator. Her fifth poetry collection *Deformations* was shortlisted for the T.S. Eliot Prize, and her translation of Maria Stepanova's *In Memory of Memory* was shortlisted for the 2021 International Booker Prize and the 2022 James Tait Black Prize.

Polly Gannon is a literary translator and quilter. She holds a PhD in Russian literature from Cornell University. For many years, she has taught intersectional cultural studies, translation and poetry. She lives in Berlin.

Peter Gizzi's recent books include *Now It's Dark, Sky Burial* and *Archeophonics*, which was a finalist for the National Book Award for Poetry.

Lindsey Hilsum is *Channel 4 News'* international editor, and the author of two books: *In Extremis: The Life of War Correspondent Marie Colvin* and *Sandstorm: Libya in the Time of Revolution*.

Rebecca May Johnson's first book is *Small Fires: An Epic in the Kitchen*. She earned a PhD in contemporary german literature from UCL for her study of Barbara Köhler's reworking of the *Odyssey*, *Niemands Frau*.

Rattawut Lapcharoensap is the author of *Sightseeing*, a collection of short stories. He lives in the central Hudson Valley and teaches at Sarah Lawrence College.

Janet Malcolm (1934–2021) was a staff writer for the *New Yorker* and the author of many books, including *In the Freud Archives*, *The Journalist and the Murderer*, *Psychoanalysis: The Impossible Profession* and *The Silent Woman: Sylvia Plath and Ted Hughes*.

Sarah Moss is the author of eight novels including *The Fell*, *Summerwater* and *Ghost Wall*. She was born in Glasgow, grew up in the north of England and now lives in Ireland, where she teaches on the MFA and MA creative writing programmes at University College Dublin.

George Prochnik was awarded a Guggenheim Fellowship in general non-fiction in 2021. He has written for publications such as the *New Yorker* and the *LA Review of Books*, and is editor-at-large for *Cabinet* magazine. 'Talk America' is an edited excerpt from *I Dream with Open Eyes*, forthcoming from Counterpoint Press.

Volodymyr Rafeyenko is a Ukrainian writer, poet, translator and critic. He initially wrote entirely in Russian, but following the outbreak of Russian aggression in 2014 he switched to Ukrainian.

Mondegreen: Songs about Death and Love is his first novel in Ukrainian. He is the Ukrainian translator of Nobel Prize winner Svetlana Alexievich's *War's Unwomanly Face*.

Suzanne Scanlon is the author of *Her 37th Year, An Index* and *Promising Young Women*. 'The Moving Target of Being' is an excerpt from her work in progress, a hybrid memoir forthcoming from Vintage/Anchor in the US and John Murray in the UK.

Dizz Tate has been published in the *Stinging Fly*, the *Tangerine* and *No Tokens Journal*, among others. Her first novel, *Brutes*, will be published in early 2023.

Daniel Trilling is a journalist and author who writes for the *Guardian*, the *London Review of Books* and others. His book about Europe's refugee crisis, *Lights in the Distance*, won Italy's 'Libri contro la fame' literary prize and was shortlisted for the 2019 Bread and Roses Award for Radical Publishing.

Sana Valiulina was born in Tallinn, in Soviet Estonia. She studied Norwegian at Moscow State University before moving to Amsterdam in 1989. She received the Jan Hanlo Essay Prize in 2017. Her latest novel, *To Grab a Wolf by the Ears* (2021), is about the Roman emperor Tiberius. She writes in Dutch and Russian.